NOWHERE?

By Aaron Marc Stein

NOWHERE?
BODY SEARCH
LEND ME YOUR EARS
COFFIN COUNTRY
LOCK AND KEY
THE FINGER
ALP MURDER
KILL IS A FOUR-LETTER WORD
SNARE ANDALUCIAN
DEADLY DELIGHT
I FEAR THE GREEKS
BLOOD ON THE STARS
HOME AND MURDER
NEVER NEED AN ENEMY
SITTING UP DEAD
MOONMILK AND MURDER
DEATH MEETS 400 RABBITS
THE DEAD THING IN THE POOL
MASK FOR MURDER
PISTOLS FOR TWO
SHOOT ME DACENT
FRIGHTENED AMAZON
THREE—WITH BLOOD
THE SECOND BURIAL
DAYS OF MISFORTUNE
THE CRADLE AND THE GRAVE
WE SAW HIM DIE
DEATH TAKES A PAYING GUEST
. . . AND HIGH WATER
THE CASE OF THE ABSENT-MINDED PROFESSOR
ONLY THE GUILTY
THE SUN IS A WITNESS
HER BODY SPEAKS
SPIRALS

NOWHERE?

AARON MARC STEIN

PUBLISHED FOR THE CRIME CLUB BY
DOUBLEDAY & COMPANY, INC.
GARDEN CITY, NEW YORK
1978

All of the characters in this book are fictitious, and any resemblance to actual persons, living or dead, is purely coincidental.

Library of Congress Cataloging in Publication Data

Stein, Aaron Marc, 1906–
  Nowhere?
  I. Title.
PZ3.S819No   [PS3569.T34]   813'.5'2
ISBN: 0-385-13065-1
Library of Congress Catalog Card Number 77-76268

Copyright © 1978 by Aaron Marc Stein
All Rights Reserved
Printed in the United States of America
First Edition

*For
Joe Hagen
because
he thinks hitchhikers would
be better for the healthful
exercise of walking.*

NOWHERE?

I.

At first sight she might have been nothing special, just another figure in the half-mile frieze of them that lined the roadside. At first sight, in fact, she was the least spectacular of the lot, nothing so conspicuous as the one who stood flanked by great piles of household goods or the one with the Saint Bernard dog and a basket brimful of Saint Bernard puppies. This one didn't even have a backpack or a guitar.

She did have a sign, but that might have been nothing, since they all had signs.

    PHILADELPHIA
    PITTSBURGH
    CLEVELAND
    DETROIT
    CHICAGO
    ST. LOUIS
    DENVER
    LOS ANGELES
    SAN FRANCISCO
    ANYWHERE
    NOWHERE

NOWHERE? I just caught it as I went cruising by and I couldn't believe it. I slowed down, slid Baby into reverse, and rolled back for a second look. You could call it an automotive double-take.

NOWHERE. That was it. That was where she wanted to go and she was standing there at the side of the road holding up her sign and waiting for someone to come along and offer her the lift that would take her there.

"I'd like to help," I said, "but I guess it's no good since I am going somewhere."

"I don't mind," she said. "It'd be your destination, not mine."

"Is that 'Move on, brother'?"

"No," she said. "It's 'Thank you very much and I don't mind if I do.'"

I leaned across to open the car door for her, but she wasn't waiting for any of that. Vaulting the door, she made a neat landing in the seat beside me. It was at that moment I first began taking notice of the girl herself. Prior to that I'd hardly been seeing her past her sign.

My first thought might have been that the kid was in shape, but it quickly came to me that she was shapely as well. She was wearing the uniform—tight jeans and loose T-shirt—and she was young enough so that on her it looked good. Young enough was all right, but I no sooner had her in the car than the thought struck me that this could be *too* young. Eighteen makes the big legal difference. It could be a lot less hazardous for guys if the visible difference was commensurate. It isn't, not ever, and least of all when they're small and trim and athletic in some mysterious way that doesn't let the muscles show. Take one that type. It may be anything from sixteen to twenty.

"Getting nowhere has never been my style," I said. "I wouldn't know how to start."

She shrugged it off.

"You just go where you're going," she said. "Maybe I'll go there with you. Maybe I'll drop off someplace along the way."

"Either way, it won't be nowhere."

"That won't matter."

"So what was with that sign of yours?" I asked.

"If you haven't anywhere to go," she said, "where do you head for? Nowhere."

"Going nowhere is staying put. It's making no move at all."

She sighed.

"That's what they're always telling me. No matter how far or how fast you run, you can't run away from yourself."

"You're running away?"

"Far and fast. It's the story of my life."

I decided I had no need to worry. It might have been a crazy line of thought, but it had some measure of mad maturity to it. The teenies don't juggle words that way.

"Do you always travel this light?" I asked.

"When you're going nowhere, you take nothing."

"And when you land somewhere without even a spare shirt to your back?"

"I can always buy a shirt."

"Standing back there, did you expect to be picked up?"

"I've never missed."

"With that same sign?"

"I print up a fresh one each time."

"Saying something different?"

"If I want something different. When I haven't anywhere to go, it says 'nowhere.'"

"You haven't anywhere to go? What about home?"

"Home? What's that?"

"It's where you hang your hat."

"I've never had a hat."

"It's where your heart is."

"My heart," she said, "is a lump of muscle that sits in my chest and squeezes on some valves to make them open and shut in a regular rhythm. Anytime it would be out of there and off someplace else, I'd be in trouble."

"And you're not in trouble now?"

"I don't think so. You don't look like trouble. You look like you'd like to be, but you won't."

I didn't know whether she intended it for a compliment or an insult. I asked.

Maybe I had an answer. I'm not at all certain of what I had.

"You're civilized," she said, "and you have a subtle mind."

"The kind of trouble I thought you were talking about, minds don't make it. It's the body you've got to watch."

"A civilized man's subtle mind keeps his body under control. He wishes it didn't, but it does."

"With only the one moment to look me over before you jumped into the car, you knew all that about me?"

"Before that," she said. "The way you reacted to my sign. There are only two kinds of men who stop when they see it—ones who are too stupid to be frightened of it, and ones who are too bright not to feel the challenge of it. It didn't take me more than a moment to know you weren't stupid."

"Want to tell me what you're running away from?"

"Not overwhelmingly."

"Mind telling me, since I'm taking a civilized, subtle interest?"

"Sorry," she said. "I didn't mean that to hurt. I should have known that it would. You'd like to come on all animal."

"I can't tell whether you're putting me on or putting me off," I said.

"Neither," she said. "It's just that it isn't interesting. I'm running away from defeat, from loss, from emptiness."

"Let's try it the other way. *Who* are you running away from?"

She laughed.

"Last time I started off for nowhere," she said, "it was an English professor picked me up. He tried the same questions but he said, 'Whom are you running away from?' I liked that 'whom.' It has a portentous sound. Whom, womb, tomb, doom—all those *oom* words—they go echoing through your soul."

"Boom, broom, and bloom," I said.

"Loom and gloom."

"What about groom?"

"As in horses or as in bride?"

"Take your pick," I said.

"I did and I lost. I'm not running away from him. I'm running away from being a loser. I had nobody to run away from. He'd already left me."

"Husband?"

"Bell, book, and candle, not to speak of blood test, banns, and license. The whole bit. We were that square."

"Divorced?" I asked.

Up to that point her answers, whether they were responsive or not, had all been prompt and glib. This time she stopped to think.

"That," she said, "could be what I'm running away from. If he can't find me, he can't divorce me."

"Don't count on it. It might be considered grounds. It's called desertion."

"I know, even though he did walk out first. Not being there in case he comes back, I guess that's desertion."

"If you stay away long enough," I said, "I'd think it would be."

"And I'd be divorced, and if they couldn't find me to tell me, I'd never have to think that I was, and I could feel as though it hadn't happened."

"That doesn't seem very satisfactory," I said.

"Maybe you've never noticed, being a man and all, but life isn't very satisfactory."

"I've noticed. You try to make the best of it."

"And you always have the choice of making the best of it or making the worst of it, and you have to be a fool not to make the best of it. And that's the end of today's lesson."

With that she shut her eyes and went to sleep. Sleeping she looked like a baby. Seeing her that way started me thinking again about the sixteen-year-olds who pass for twenty and about all the state lines we'd be crossing if she went on riding with me through the rest of the day. Since we'd crossed one at the very beginning, I told myself it was too late to be worrying about any of that.

She was nobody's knock-you-dead beauty. The body was good—maybe not great, but good. A little less spare and a little less hard would have been better, but that didn't make it anything a man could find repulsive. The face was what I'd call serviceable. From moment to moment it was what she made it. Smiling, she could look open and easy. Feeling ugly was all it took to make her look ugly. It was an interesting face. There was never any telling what it would be doing next.

She slept for a long time and I drove. I might just as well

have been rolling along alone. Baby is a Porsche, and you know how it is with sports cars. There are those bucket seats and they are the twentieth-century equivalent of an earlier era's bundling board. They make all the difference between nearness and closeness. Without the individual cradling those seats provide, she might have been snuggled up against me. Her head might have been pillowed on my shoulder. Some of the preliminaries might have been taking care of themselves. As it was, I was giving her nothing but transportation—or so it seemed to me.

We were well into evening before she woke and we had a good four hundred miles behind us. Whether it was four hundred miles nearer nowhere or not, I didn't know. I was thinking that while she slept I could have turned around and driven back to where I'd picked her up. I was wondering how she would have taken that, discovering that for all the riding she'd done, she'd gone nowhere. I was almost wishing I didn't have places to go and that I had the time for that kind of acting out on her word game.

The motels along the road had begun to show NO VACANCY signs. That's always the warning signal. You want to quit before they'll all be like that and you'll end up with no place to lay your head. I pushed on, but I was looking for a place as I went. Apart from the fleabags, motels are all much the same. I was going to make do with the first one that said VACANCY and looked as though they changed the sheets.

It wasn't long before we hit one. I pulled in and turned off the motor. It was as though with the turning of the ignition key I had triggered some eyelid-lifting mechanism. Her eyes opened and instantaneously she was full awake. There wasn't even a moment's hesitation for going through any where-am-I-and-who-are-you routine. She took me in and she took in our surroundings.

"For me," she said, "this will mean one of two things. If it isn't 'Take off, Baby,' it'll be 'Take it off, Baby.'"

"*You* call it," I told her.

"And you don't care one way or the other? No preference?"

"That subtle and civilized mind has the animal under control."

"You can let the animal off the leash, but only if you want to."

"I want to."

"So do I. You're nice."

I left her in the car and went into the office. There was just a kid in there holding down the desk. He had the sulky look a boy gets when he's been waiting too long for the adolescent acne to clear up. He was trying to conceal it under a beard, but he was doing himself no good. He was much better at raising pimples than he was at raising whiskers.

I asked for a double and he told me he could let me have one with two double beds. That's something I've never understood about motels. In my arithmetic that would be a double double, but you don't understand motels. You just make do with them. I've always wanted to ask whether the charge would be the same if two people used only one of the beds or if they used a half of each, but he didn't seem the one to ask. I said it would do us.

He shoved the registration card at me and, while I signed it and filled it out, he was quoting me the rate and telling me that 11 A.M. was checkout time. I won't say the kid was particularly relaxed about the way I registered. Motels are like that. If a guest is using a credit card, they'll want the signature on the registration card to match the credit card signature. Whichever way the guest is paying, they want the make of his car and the license number. Beyond that they don't care. Just the one name does it. No need for any Mr.-and-Mrs. fakery.

He handed me the key and told me it was Number 15, first door to the left of the office. When I came out, the girl was standing beside the car waiting for me. I pointed out the room and handed her the key. She unlocked the door and went in while I was moving Baby to her parking slot. When I came into the room, the girl was in the bathroom.

She wasn't in there long and she made great use of the time she took. She came out looking astonishingly changed. It was the same jeans and the same T-shirt. It had to be. She had nothing else with her, but it was something she had done with her hair. She had managed a dressed-for-the-evening look, and I don't mean a bedroom look.

"I'm hungry," she said. "Can I take you out to dinner?"

"No."

"I thought, since I had to proposition you, it could wait maybe till we had some food in us."

"I'm beginning to understand your husband," I said.

"You may think so, but you're not. When he couldn't wait, he went elsewhere. That was a lot of what was wrong with us."

I let that lay. Saying nothing, I peeled out of my jacket and shirt and ducked into the bathroom for a wash. I hit my bag for a fresh shirt. I shrugged back into the jacket.

"Then we do eat?" she asked.

"I take you to dinner."

"If your masculine self-image needs to have it that way," she said. "It's good for your self-esteem and for my pocket."

The jacket didn't feel right. When Caraceni builds you a jacket, it feels like a second skin. I don't mean it fits you that tight, but only that the feel of it on your back is so natural it could be a part of you. Now it was feeling just a shade off balance. It couldn't be that I had changed, not just in the few minutes I'd been washing up. The change had to be in the jacket, and there was only one possibility. There had been some shift in the distribution of an item or items in the pocket. I patted the pockets. On the very first pat I located the misplacement. My billfold was missing from the pocket that had always been its home. That pocket had been left empty and the billfold had been crowded into the pocket that held my sunglasses.

I brought it out of there and, with the girl watching me, I checked it out. Not having anything like an exact tally on the number of bucks I'd been carrying, I couldn't check it down to the penny or even down to the dollar, but the amount I found in there seemed right, or at least so close to it that anything that might have been taken couldn't have been more than a dollar or two. Otherwise it was driver's license and credit cards and such. Everything seemed to be there.

I looked from the billfold to the girl. I didn't have to say anything. She read the question in my look.

"Yes, Matthew Erridge," she said, waving one of my cards at me. "I checked it out. You never introduced yourself, and I had to have something to call you. Also I'd put you in a spot where you felt you had to buy me dinner. I wasn't going to let you do it if I saw you couldn't afford it."

"Satisfied that a hamburger isn't going to tip me over into bankruptcy?"

"Satisfied," she said. "You can even go for a side of french fries."

It was feeble. I saw no way I could believe it, but then I could think of no answer that would have seemed more rational. I told myself that this was not a rational kid. She'd been headed for nowhere. Who was to say that she hadn't already arrived?

"Okay," I said. "Let's go."

We started out to the car. Before climbing aboard, she dropped her hand on my arm and held me up for a moment.

"You're a great guy, Matthew," she said. "It could be easy to love you."

"Good," I said. "I wouldn't want you to have to strain yourself."

"No strain."

She took my head in her hands and bent it to bring my lips within reach. She kissed me, and there was nothing wrong with it except that I've never been the passive type. I took her in my arms and I kissed her. She wasn't the passive type either. A moment or two earlier, before we'd come out of the room, it would have wiped out all thoughts of dinner, or at the least it would have postponed them. Even as it was, for a moment I was thinking I might switch about and take her back in. I pushed the thought away. Her timing was too good. I had the feeling that I was being manipulated.

My right hand found its way to the regulation target and I handed her a couple of light whacks.

"Behave yourself," I said, "or you'll find yourself going to bed without your supper."

"Yes, Daddy," she said.

Nothing could have been more demure than the way she settled herself in the car.

We took off.

"I haven't had a chance to go through your pockets," I said. "So what do I call you?"

"How would you like 'Lolita'?"

"I wouldn't. Whether I'm Humbert Humbert or the other guy, I wouldn't."

"Maybe my mother shouldn't have read the book, though I think she went to the movie."

"If she read the book or saw the movie, she wouldn't have called you Lolita. Mothers aren't like that."

She shrugged.

"I wouldn't know what mothers are like," she said. "I never had but one, and I've never been able to figure what she was like."

"When you have a daughter, what are you going to call her?"

"If I have a daughter, Matthew, I'll name her after you."

"A girl called Matthew?"

"Do people call you Matthew? I should think it would be Matt or Matty."

"Matt."

"See? I can call her Matt, short for Mathilda."

"Is it going to bother you much if I don't believe you?" I asked.

"Not much."

We were in western Pennsylvania and in a part of it I didn't know. Picking a place to eat was going to have to be a guess and a gamble. I was hoping to spot a joint where the parking lot would be moderately well filled and where the license plates on the parked cars would, to at least some fair degree, be local. It's always possible that the local taste in feeding might be terrible, but if it's a spot the locals frequent, you know that you at least have a place that is to somebody's taste.

What I found had a no-nonsense bar and an unambitious but solid menu. They did steaks and, from what I could see on the tables we passed, they did them well.

The kid said no to a drink. So while I was working on my Virginia Gentleman and water, she had nothing to divert her from working on me. It was as it had been outside the motel room. She snuggled. She pawed. She nibbled my ear. She all but climbed all over me. I can't say I didn't enjoy it, but I also can't say I was comfortable with it.

We were too much on display and there wasn't a soul in the place who was missing out on the show. Those who were seated where they could watch shoveled steak into their mouths mechanically while they kept their eyes fixed on Lolita and me. The unluckier ones who were seated with their backs to us just turned in their seats and gawped.

So what was there to see?

A guy who just sat there sucking on a whiskey while he was in the process of getting raped? Could I leave it at that? On the other hand, was I left with any initiative at all? There was nothing I could exercise without getting us thrown out of the place, and the kid had said she was hungry. I knew *I* was.

When the steaks came, she simmered down. She was indeed hungry. The food that was put in front of her took some of her attention, but not all of it. From time to time she took a breather, stuff like hand-feeding me french fries she took off her plate.

It was obvious that the locals had never seen anything like it. I saw one woman pick up her plate and change her seat. She didn't want to miss anything. I was uncomfortably aware of our audience. The kid wasn't unaware, but the difference was that she wasn't uncomfortable with it. I had the nasty feeling that she might have been carrying on more for their benefit than for mine.

It got to the place where all this stuff that should have been making me amorous was having the opposite effect. It was turning me off. The kid wasn't playing up to me, she was playing me. I wondered whether, when she told me I could call her Lolita, she hadn't been giving me fair warning. Maybe I didn't have enough years on me to have been her father, but I wasn't lacking them by much. In her eyes I could have been lacking them not at all. I was, after all, an old man. I had to shave every day.

I had coffee and a drink while she worked on a dessert. It was an ice cream thing that swam in hot chocolate syrup and was mounded high with chopped nuts and whipped cream. From her first sight of it, it cut her down to what might have been her proper age. She became a little girl for whom passion didn't mean sex. It meant hot fudge and whipped cream.

She tucked into it. When she had lapped up the last gooey drops and, after considering another and reluctantly deciding that she couldn't go it, she went off to the little girl's room. (There are vast areas of this great country of ours where it's never called anything else. Nobody's ever told me what the adults are supposed to do.)

I had some more coffee and another drink while I waited for her. She was gone a long time. I don't know how long I would have sat there waiting for her or how many drinks it would have been before I either passed out or came to my senses. I didn't have to hang on and find out. The waitress came over and settled it for me. Perhaps she had never been told that it isn't good restaurant manners to bring a man his check before he's asked for it, or maybe it was that she thought she had something for me and that I should be having it without further delay.

It was a sealed envelope. I studied it before I opened it. It was addressed to me. I ripped it open. It contained two grubby and beat-up tens and a sheet of the restaurant's letterhead. I couldn't help being aware of the waitress. She was watching me while I read the note. It was brief. It took almost no time to read it, although it took far longer to understand it.

"Dear Matt," she had written. "You are a dear. It would have been nice. Thinking about me, you will be thinking what I wish you wouldn't, but it's no good asking you not to think it, since there's nothing else you could possibly think, because I am anything you think I am. This is a dirty trick and I know it. Try to believe that I didn't start with anything like this in mind. I didn't plan it this way. This is the last thing I could have thought might happen, but it has happened. The money? It's not an insult, Matt, and it's not a castration. It's just the only way I have of letting you know I wasn't playing you along for the dinner. I can't pretend I wasn't playing you along, but it wasn't for that. I'll never forget you. You are always going to be one of the nice things that happened to me. So try not to despise me too much."

She had signed it "Lolita."

My first impulse was to tear the note up and the two damn tens with it, but the waitress hadn't moved off. She was there right beside me and she was watching me with what I took to be clinical interest.

My second thought was to give her the two tens as a tip, but both thoughts had no more than surfaced before I was rejecting them. I was sitting there under that clinical inspection. I didn't care to furnish a case history that would be any meatier than had already been provided. I folded the two tens inside the note, returned all of it to the envelope, and stuck the envelope in my pocket. For paying the check and tipping the waitress, I went into my billfold.

She thanked me for the tip, but she wasn't leaving it at that.

"If you're going to be lonely," she said, "I get through here at ten-thirty."

This wasn't your ordinary solicitation. This one dripped with pity. I couldn't take it.

"Do you think you could afford me?" I said. "I don't come cheap. Those bills you were looking at, they're my minimum fee. I gave her a bargain rate."

That took care of the waitress. It wiped out her pity. She took off in a hurry. I did the long walk out of the restaurant. There wasn't an eye in the place that didn't follow me all the way to the door. I had been thinking that once I was out of the place it would stop, but outside there was the boy who parked the cars.

He took off without a word, but when he came back with the Porsche he was wearing a worried scowl.

"Gee, mister," he said. "I thought she'd be waiting in the car. I don't know where she went. I looked all over and she isn't back there, not anywhere back there."

"Who?" I asked, as though I didn't know.

I was curious, though, since it seemed to me that there would have to have been something to make this kid think she would be there waiting in the car.

"The young lady," the boy said, "the one who came with you. She came out and she asked me where I parked the car. I said I'd get it, figuring you were on your way and just stopped to pay the check and like that, and I'd have it out here and not hold you up. But she said no. She said just tell her where I had it. She only wanted something out of it. She went out back and I haven't seen her since. I thought sure she was in the car waiting."

I told the kid it was all right, but I was wondering what she could possibly have wanted out of the Porsche. The glove compartment was locked, and anything of mine I'd left there was locked up in it. I couldn't imagine it could have been anything of hers, since she'd had nothing but what she stood up in.

As soon as the kid was out of the car, however, and I was behind the wheel, I knew what she'd gone for. There had been that one thing of hers she'd left in the car. It was her NOWHERE sign. She had left it on the seat. It wasn't there any more.

Of course it was crazy, but I half expected that once I was out of the restaurant driveway and on the road, I'd find her with her sign. It made no sense. Nobody driving past in the dark was going to be able to read it, but then, had this babe ever made sense?

I pulled out of the driveway. If she had stationed herself anywhere along the road, she had already picked up a fresh hitch, or she had walked far enough to put herself out of sight. I drove. Without any thought about where I was going, I drove fast and far. I was blowing off steam. I was telling myself that the last place I wanted to go would be that motel room with the two double beds. But then, I didn't like the idea of any other motel room either and I'd left my suitcase back in that one.

After something near two hours of aimless speeding I began thinking of myself as too much like Lolita, if that was her name. I was coming around to thinking of myself as another freaked-out nut hell-bent for nowhere. I turned Baby around and drove back the way I'd come. I'd cooled down some by then, so I drove without pushing so hard.

Since I'd wandered a long way, it was well past one before I was back at the motel. I'd expected that the place would be all dark. Motels don't keep night clerks on all-night duty. They had the NO VACANCY sign lit up, and that made it all the more astonishing that there should be a light in the office and that the kid who'd checked me in should still be up to observe my arrival.

He remained in the office. I parked Baby and went straight into the room. The drinks I'd had in the restaurant were now far enough in the past so that I was having the ebb tide on whatever it might have been they had done for me. I had a bottle in my bag and the tap water was running good and cold. I was all right for Bourbon and branch, and I didn't need ice. Even if I'd wanted it, I'd have made do without it. That wakeful kid in the office had seen enough.

I poured myself a good slug of the whiskey and wetted it down just a little with the cold water out of the bathroom tap. I kicked out of my shoes and pulled my tie loose. I was just settling in with my drink when there was a knock at the door.

Lolita having a change of mind?

That was every way unlikely. She would need to have had a lift from the restaurant, and there could be no explaining the precision of the timing. Certainly she hadn't had a lift to follow me all the way to wherever it was I'd been and back.

I opened the door. It was the kid out of the office. Since I'd planted myself in the doorway, any seeing in he was going to do would have to be around my edges. He tried and he didn't have the grace to be anything less than obvious about it.

"Something bothering you?" I asked.

"I'm going to bed," he said.

"Need somebody to listen to your prayers and tuck you in?"

"I thought I'd check first in case I could get you something you needed."

"Like what?"

"Like I got numbers I can call."

"For what?"

"You know. After all, you're paying for a double."

"That's *my* department," I said, and I slammed the door shut.

I felt it hit up against him as it slammed, and I heard him gasp as the breath exploded out of him. With my mind more on him than on what I was doing, I tossed off my drink. So then I had finished it without taking any pleasure in it, and I had to make myself another just for the enjoyment.

Eventually I skinned out of my clothes and hit the bed. Maybe I slept and maybe I fell into a drunken stupor. Whichever it was, it was solid and deep. Waking from it was a slow, dazed climb back up to consciousness.

My first awareness was only of a light, a single highbeam. I asked myself how a man was to know whether it was a motorcycle or a car with one of its headlights gone. Before I could begin to give myself an answer to that one, another question confronted me.

Whether a motorcycle or a car, what would it be doing in my motel room?

Since you are presumably neither half asleep nor dragging yourself up out of an alcoholic stupor, you already know that it wasn't a motorcycle or a car. It was a visitor with a flashlight. It was, in fact, a visitor who had already accomplished the purpose of the visit and was in the process of withdrawing.

The time it took me to come full awake was no more than a matter of a second or two, but it was sufficient for an intruder, already on the way out, to make it to the door. The flashlight had been switched off and it had become a matter of hearing more than seeing. I heard the door open and I came charging off the bed. I can't say I had anything specific in mind. Since there was no time for arriving at considered conclusions, I was leaping into action without plan or thought. I had been invaded. I was going to jump the intruder and nab him before he could get away.

I jumped and came up hard against something that shouldn't have been there. It caught me just below the knees. My momentum carrying the rest of me forward, I toppled and landed draped in a face-down sprawl over the back and arms of an easy chair.

That chair was where it should never have been. What with its unexpected and inexplicable location and the peculiarity of my encounter with it, I couldn't in the dark work up any immediate recognition of what it was. Who carries around with him a memory of chairs that would include what it feels like to be seated in one wrong side to?

There was a lot of it and it was blocking me. Again, it couldn't have been more than a second or two that it had me baffled, but I did have to haul myself out of the chair and find my way around it to head toward the door. Furthermore, I now had to feel my way toward the door. Having tangled with one unseen obstacle, I was now imagining that another would be looming and another and another every step of the way.

I made it and I yanked the door open. Outside there was a little more light than in the room. The moon was shining through a thin cloud cover. By its light I could see no one. Any number of guys could have been lurking in the shadows but, for what reason I didn't know, I had a feeling that the shadows were empty.

While I stood out there looking one way and another, I heard the sound of a car starting up, and the nearness of it was confirmed when I could hear the whisper of the tires and the diminishing sound as it pulled away. I only heard it. I never saw it at all.

I started for the Porsche to give chase, digging for my car

keys as I went. Finding myself with no place to dig, I was pulled up short. I had no pockets because I had no pants, not even the pocketless kind that come in pajamas. When I'd finished my drinking, I had dropped into bed. I'd undressed while doing the drinking and I'd dropped off buck naked. So now I was out under that veiled moon exposing my unveiled butt to the night air.

Obviously, even if I was going to give chase that way, I couldn't get started till I went back in the room for the car keys and, since in all probability it was already too late, by then it would be impossible, and that wasn't even considering any need for jumping into pants before taking to the highway.

Bowing to the inevitable, I headed back to the room. Need I tell you? In the heat of my pursuit I had let the door shut behind me. I was locked out.

The window was open but only behind a good solid screen. Taking the screen out with nothing, even so much as a pocketknife, to work with would be a noisy job. It might be less noisy perhaps than breaking the door down, but noisy enough to rouse the occupants of all the other rooms. Although I've never been unduly uptight in the male-modesty department, I did feel I wasn't suitably dressed for rousing everybody. There was a bell on the office door. I leaned on that.

I was a long time leaning on it. That kid who had been holding down the office, having rented every last one of his units and having tried me on his side line and rung up a no-sale there, had evidently gone to bed. He seemed to be a sound sleeper or at least a slow waker. It was more than ten minutes of working that bell before I got any action. I knew exactly how long it was, because I exaggerated a bit when I said I was locked out with nothing on. I wasn't totally naked. I was wearing my watch and I kept checking it. It had been ten minutes after three when I'd first applied myself to the bell. It was twenty-two after when the lights came up in the office and the kid emerged from a back room, rubbing his eyes with one hand while he zipped up his pants with the other.

Seeing me through the glass panel of the office door, he stopped and stared. He forgot the zipper and left it at half mast.

I was in no spot for criticising that. Compared to me, he was overdressed. He hesitated. For a moment he half turned away, looking as though he were about to go back to bed without doing anything about me. Then he turned back, but only to stand and steal glances at me.

Maybe he was trying to convince himself that he was really awake, or maybe he was trying to get up the courage to open the office door. After all, I had to recognize that from where he stood he could have been thinking he had the problem of a raving maniac on his hands. There were all sorts of possibilities on what might have been going through his head, and for a moment I had the thought that there might also be the possibility that he was just putting on an act, that he hadn't been asleep at all, that he had been the intruder in my room. He had the means. He would have a key. But then, there had been that car I'd heard start up and drive away.

I went into sign language. I pointed toward the door to my room. I pantomimed turning a key in a lock. Slowly he moved toward the office door. I worked at looking peaceable. I didn't know how I could go about looking sane.

He opened the door a crack and stood back of it, ready to slam it shut if I made even the first peculiar move. I got a foot in the door, thinking even as I did it that it would be better with a shoe on but hoping the kid wouldn't do anything savage.

"I woke up to find a burglar in my room," I said. "I chased him and got myself locked out."

The kid blinked.

"Burglar?" he mumbled. "What burglar?"

"I don't know what burglar. He was on his way out when I woke. He was gone before I could get to him."

"How did he get in?"

"I don't know how he got in. I guess he was better off than me. He had his pants on, so he probably had a key in his pants pocket."

"A key to your room? *You* have the key to your room."

"Yes." I worked at being patient. "And it's locked inside the room. There must be a duplicate or a master key."

"I've got those, the duplicate and the master."

"Good. That's what I thought. So sometime before daybreak you can let me back into my room."

He went off. I hoped it was to get the key. He made no move to shut the office door against me. I realized that it could be because of my foot, but I wanted to take it for an encouraging sign. I moved into the office and took myself behind the registration desk. I was there when he returned with the key. Seeing me, he scowled.

"What are you doing back there?" he demanded.

"Cover," I said. "Concealment. You don't think I need it?"

"Mister," the kid said, "I think you're out of your skull."

"Also possible," I told him.

That much of an admission seemed to do wonders for him. He gained confidence. He took command. He even snapped out an order.

"Stay where you are," he said. "I'll bring you your pants."

That wasn't too unreasonable. I waited. It was only a moment or two before he was back with my slacks. He handed them over the counter. I stayed back there while I pulled them on and zipped them up. He moved back to the room door and waited there, holding it open for me.

I thanked him and apologized for waking him. He disregarded all of that. He waited till I was back in the room. Then he shut the door and stood with his back against it, still waiting.

"I'll be all right now," I said. "Thanks again."

"You had a burglar. What did he take?"

"I don't know. I haven't looked yet."

"Look."

It didn't take much looking. I hadn't done any neat job with my clothes when I'd taken them off. They were lying wherever I'd dropped them. Though I can't say I had any exact memory of where I'd dropped each garment as I'd taken it off, things were lying in places where they might have naturally fallen. Nothing looked as though it had been disturbed—nothing, that is, but the big easy chair. That had been moved. It had been shifted to a place in the room where nobody would ever put a chair unless it was with the purpose of setting up an obstacle between the beds and the rest of the room.

My watch was on me. I explored my pants pockets for all the stuff I usually carry there. I had all of it. I picked up my jacket and checked the pockets. There was no missing item there. I checked my billfold. Since it hadn't been taken, I was assuming it would have been emptied of whatever money I'd had in it. I had no question in my mind that the intruder had already been on his way out when I first woke. It couldn't have been that I had interrupted him before he'd had time to grab anything.

But he had taken nothing from my billfold. There was only one other place to look. In the pocket along with the billfold there was that envelope with the note and the two tens. I pulled out the note. Nothing else came with it. That grubby pair of ten-dollar bills had been taken, just those and nothing else. The kid was standing there watching my every move.

"Get much?" he asked.

"Nothing," I said.

I wasn't about to tell him about the two tens or to try to explain them.

"You're sure you had a burglary?" he asked.

Of course I was sure and I was about to say so, but that wasn't going to speed my getting rid of the guy.

"Either I dreamt it, or I woke and went after him before he could grab anything," I said.

"You dreamt."

If I was going to settle for a phony explanation, my preference lay with the other suggested possibility. It was less damaging to my self-esteem.

"The chair," I said. "He moved it so it would be in my way in case I woke up. I didn't dream that and it didn't move itself."

"Yeah," the kid said.

He wasn't believing a word of it. I slipped him a bill. If it didn't help him toward belief, it helped him find his way out of the room.

II.

Both by my watch and by the way I was feeling, I still had a lot of sleeping to do. I threw myself on the bed and made a try at it. It was no good. I ached for it but I couldn't get it made. My mind was racing. It wasn't getting anywhere, but it just wouldn't simmer down. After about a half hour of fighting my eyelids, trying to keep them shut when they had developed a will of their own, I gave up on it.

I got up and showered and dressed. A few minutes after four I took to the road again. I drove through the dawn and the sunrise. The earliest of the going-to-work traffic joined me on the roads. Now those recalcitrant eyelids were taking over again. This time they wouldn't hold up. I was fighting against their closing. I pulled in at a truck stop and worked on a trucker's breakfast.

Steak and eggs, fried potatoes, countless cups of strong, black coffee—it should have been enough to hand me a new charge of energy. Back on the road I quickly learned better. All that breakfast and all that coffee had done nothing for me. If I had been in a state of stupidity before, now it was that I was stupid and stuffed. I had to pull off the road. I hit a motel and pulled up there. It took a few minutes before I could make the man in the office believe that there could be such a thing as an early-morning check-in. It may well have been more my slugged look than anything I told him that convinced him that I was looking for a place to sleep, and that I needed to do that sleeping without delay even though it was at a time when his guests of the night before were only beginning to get up.

He found a room where there had been an early departure.

The maid was in there, but he thought she was just about finished.

"She doesn't have to finish," I said. "I'll take it the way it is just so long as I can have it while I can still walk."

The man in the office was amenable, but the maid had standards. She still had this to do and that to do. The gentleman wouldn't have long to wait, but he would have to wait till she was finished doing up the room.

The gentleman told her to do as she liked and not pay any attention to him. He pushed past her mops and her brushes and started peeling out of his clothes. The maid stuck it out till pants time. Just short of their coming down, she dashed out and left the gentleman in sole possession of his room.

I fell onto the bed and into oblivion. It was a long sleep and a good sleep, dreamless and without any intervals of waking. When late that afternoon I came out of it, it wasn't because I woke. I was wakened.

First there was the knocking. Since it was no kind of knuckle job, it took me a moment or two to recognize the hammering for what it was. It was certainly more than could have been needed for rousing me. It came closer to what might have been needed for breaking the door down. They were heavy, reverberating blows. From the sound of them they could have been from a sledge or a woodman's axe.

There was also the shouting, and that was explicit enough.

"We know you're in there. Open up. Police. Come out with your hands up. We're giving you three minutes before we come in after you, and we'll come in shooting."

That brought me full awake. The pounding had wakened me. The shouted words lifted me off the bed. I could have liked those words better if they had sounded more professional. They were too shrill. They carried an edge of hysteria. If they were intended to be frightening, I could tell from the sound of them that the guy was frightening himself more than he was frightening me, and it was only because of that that I felt menaced. Men with guns can be dangerous. Frightened men with guns can't be anything else.

I shouted back. It had to be a shout if I was to be heard at all.

"I'll be right with you. Just a sec while I put my pants on."

"Never mind your pants. Open up."

On my way to the door I pulled on my shorts. I turned the doorknob and started opening the door.

"Come out with both your hands on your head."

Following instructions, I had to let go of the doorknob. Promptly the draft blew the door shut.

"No games. Come on out of there."

"No games, brother. You can't have it both ways. If I have both my hands on my head, how do I open the door? Want me to try it with my teeth?"

There were several moments of silence. We were evidently involved with an unforeseen dilemma. After a few moments, however, the orders began coming through.

I was ordered over to the window. I was told to open the curtains. I was ordered to stand at the window with my hands on my head and not to move from the window. I complied with all these instructions to the letter. I was fully confident that I had only to show myself and the whole deal would be off. They had to be hitting the wrong room. It couldn't be well-behaved, solid-citizen Matthew Erridge that they were after. Hadn't he been leading a blameless life? Just as they could see me at the window, I could see them as they were arrayed outside. Actually, I couldn't see much of them except their guns.

They were ranged in a wide circle, evidently having taken every inch of cover that offered. They were leaving as little of themselves sticking out as they could manage, but it was easy to locate them by their guns. So far as I could see, there were six of them. At least I could count that many guns, and every last one of them trained dead on me where I stood at the window.

I had expected I would be a reassuring sight or possibly a disconcerting sight, since it seemed to me that they couldn't possibly fail to perceive that they were zeroed in on the wrong quarry. From the assembled armament outside that motel room,

I couldn't imagine that they could have been after anything less than Public Enemy No. 1, armed and dangerous.

One of them came out from behind his cover. With his gun at the ready he came forward. He was a big guy with a great beer belly that hung out over his belt. As he came, he was yelling orders at his men. He was telling them to keep me covered. The words were all right, but he didn't have the tone of command. He sounded as though he were begging them to keep him safe from big bad Erridge.

He reached the door and shifted his gun to his left hand. He had a key. I could guess that he'd hit the office for it. He unlocked the door and opened it a crack.

"Stay where you are, Erridge," he barked at me. "Don't move. I'd just as soon shoot you as not."

"I'm not moving," I said. "I'd just as soon you didn't shoot me."

"Yeah," he said. "Shooting's too good for you."

He came up behind me and snapped a handcuff on my right wrist. Yanking on the cuff, he brought that hand down behind my back and held it there. Then he made a bare-hand grab at my other wrist, yanked that down behind my back, and snapped the cuff on that one.

Hauling hard on the cuffs while he aimed a kick at my ankles, he kicked my feet out from under me and slammed me flat to the floor.

Steaming? Of course I was, but at the same time I was relishing my anticipation of the moment when this big-bellied lug would learn better and would start sweating. Nobody sweats like a fat man.

"Now that you've got me where I can't possibly hurt you," I said, "suppose you tell me what this is all about and what the hell you think you're doing."

Fatso launched into a rapid-fire routine. He was zipping out the words as fast as he could flip them off his tongue. Have you ever heard a kid recite a memorized piece? He has it down perfectly and he doesn't understand a word of it. He makes all the right sounds but he throws them at you, all run together into gibberish. That was the way my fat captor was doing it, and he'd gone through a lot of it before I realized that he was reading me my rights.

I heard him out. It was obvious that he was going to go through the whole of his memorized piece. There wasn't a chance of making sense with him until he had finished his recitation. I had little confidence that there would be much chance of it even then, but I was going to try. I hadn't failed to notice that he'd addressed me by name and that he had the name right. That was ominous.

During the recitation his cohorts came filtering into the room. They ranged themselves around us with their guns leveled at me. They were all younger than the head man, but not so young that they hadn't yet started on their beer bellies. The way they carried their guns, I could see that they knew how to shoot. The question in my mind was, Did they know how to hold a gun without shooting it?

They had smooth, hard faces. Reading those faces when they were in repose, you could see stupidity in them and laziness. Behind the guns, they read for malice and sadism. I wondered whether they could be thinking they were dealing with so dangerous a criminal, or if it was only that they had so little experience with anything heavier than writing a traffic ticket that they would rate anything at all as big-time stuff.

Whichever, I was telling myself to play it carefully. If there was any discipline or self-control shown in this encounter, it was going to have to be mine. They had too much of the lynch-mob look about them.

By the time the head man had finished rattling off his recitation of my rights, I had chosen my words and I had them nicely lined up in my head. I had also set myself the precise tone of soft-voiced, low-keyed, patient curiosity in which I was to deliver them.

"Since I don't know what I'm supposed to have done," I said, "I wish you'd tell me."

"Suppose *you* tell *us*."

It was no kind of a request. It was a taunt.

"That you have the wrong man? Will that do any good?"

"It won't do you any good."

"Since I've done nothing, I'll be all right. What about you? Do you think it'll do you any good arresting the wrong man?"

"Your name Erridge?"

"It is."

"Matthew Erridge?"

"Right."

"You drive that snappy car?"

"The Porsche? Yes."

"And you ain't done nothing?"

"I ain't done nothing."

Maybe in my mind I was mocking him, but I was careful to let none of it leak into my look or my voice. I was telling myself that maybe if I talked to him in his own language, he might find it less difficult to understand.

"And you ain't *going* to do nothing," he said. "I'm taking the cuffs off of you long enough for you to get some clothes on before I take you in. You be smart now and don't you go trying anything, because we'd just as soon shoot you as not. You want to remember that. We'll try not to kill you. A couple of bullets in your legs like. That'll slow you down enough. So you watch it. Okay?"

"I'll watch it."

All around me, his men adjusted the level of their guns. They were bringing the aim down a little but not so much as to bring them to bear on my legs. They had their own chosen target. Call it at groin level.

He unlocked the cuffs and took them off me. As soon as he had them off, however, he backed rapidly away from me, putting his men with their leveled guns between himself and me. He was taking no chances with Mad Dog Erridge. I was to have no opportunity for grabbing at his gun or for grabbing him to shelter behind his load of lard.

From that safe distance he gave me my orders. I was to turn around and face the wall. I was to spread my arms and put my hands against the wall. I was to spread my legs. Keeping my hands on the wall and my feet spread wide, I was to edge my feet backward till I was tilted against the wall in precarious balance. If you want to have an absolute guarantee against a man's making any sudden moves while you are patting him down for weapons, you position him that way. You come up behind him and you put one foot just inside one of his. You then have him under complete control. A quick kick against his ankle will take the foot out from under him and send him crashing down on his face.

He wasn't content with having his foot in the strategic position. He worked at making me aware of its being there. He kept it pressed against mine. He didn't have much patting down to do. After all, I was naked except for my shorts. So it would be only something I might have concealed under them, and the possibilities were limited.

Within the narrow range of what little of me I had under cover, his exploration was thorough. On the feel of it, it was a toss up whether he was looking for a concealed weapon or verifying my sex. I have a hunch that it's also a process designed for inducing in a man a proper prisoner attitude. It tells him emphatically that he has lost all his options. He's at the mercy of his captors and he'd better not forget it.

Finished with those games, he again beat a retreat to a position out of the field of fire, and from that distance he told me that I could now bring my feet together. I could edge them toward the wall until I had them under me. I could turn around slowly, staying where I was against the wall.

Coming around to where I could see him, I saw that he was picking up my clothes and checking them out, working as carefully and as thoroughly on my shirt and pants and socks and shoes and jacket as he had worked on me.

He threw me the shirt and told me to put it on. He pitched me my socks. On my slacks he took a little more time. He went through the pockets, taking everything out and inspecting it before putting it back and pitching me the pants. There were only two items he held out, my pocketknife and my car keys. He set them aside along with my belt. There were no shoelaces or garters for him to worry about, and he didn't toss me my tie. The last item was my jacket. On that it was as it had been with my slacks, all pockets emptied, all contents examined and returned.

When he had me turn around and put my hands behind my back in preparation for his moving in and snapping on the handcuffs, I did as he told me, but I did speak up.

"I'm going peacefully," I said. "I can wait for you to find out that you're making a mistake. Till then I'm not going anywhere."

"You better believe you're not going anywhere," he said as he snapped the cuffs on.

With one of his men on each side of me and guns fore and aft, they hustled me out of the room and shoved me into a police car. For a highway motel well removed from any town center, it was a considerable crowd that had gathered outside to watch the capture. I caught a quick look at faces as I was being hustled past. I didn't like what I saw. The spectators were out of uniform and with no weapons on display, but apart from that, they might have been the twin brothers of my captors. There wasn't a face in the lot in which I was not seeing the lynch-mob look.

Two of the cops wedged me between them in the back seat. A third drove, and a fourth sat beside him in front—riding shotgun, I suppose. The rest of them, all but the head man, rode in a second police car. Fatso took off in solitary glory. He was driving Baby. I could have wished that she would wreck him, but the thought didn't come to me at the time. I was too much worried about the possibility that he might wreck her. It isn't often that I let anyone drive her and he would never have been the type, but obviously I had no choice.

I made a try with the lugs who were riding with me.

"Anything wrong with telling me what this is all about?" I asked.

"When you've got to be told, you'll be told."

"And till then?"

"Don't get any ideas about giving anybody a hard time."

"A hard time? I'm the most co-operative prisoner you'll ever see."

"Yeah, and don't go getting any smart-ass ideas."

They took me into a town I'd never seen before. If you're riding the superhighways, you go by hundreds of towns without ever getting to see the courthouse square in any of them. This one had some good trees dotted around its patch of scruffy lawn. The courthouse held down one side of the square. On the opposite side in similar majesty stood the post office. Each of the two other sides had a church, one flanked by a five-and-dime and a drugstore, the other by a bank and a gas station.

The jail was in a wing of the courthouse. I was driven around back and down a ramp into a basement garage where I was hustled out of the police car. Without thinking about it, I hung back a bit to see where Baby would be coming to rest. I didn't get to see much of anything. All my hanging back got me was a lusty kick in the butt.

I was hustled up a flight of stairs and flung into a cell. When the two buckos who had me by the arms heaved me up and pitched me through the cell door, the obvious intention was to dump me in there on my face. I managed just enough of a midair twist to take the fall on my shoulder. I wasn't hurt but I was burning. Hearing something behind me that sounded like a couple of chuckles didn't cool me down any.

"You want them cuffs off, you get up and come over here," one of the cops said.

If you're flat on the floor with your hands fastened behind your back, getting to your feet isn't impossible, but it does take a little doing. I was in the process of doing it when a totally unexpected hand reached down and took a grip on my arm to help me up. I shook the hand off. I was steaming and I wasn't taking anybody's help.

I got to my feet on my own.

"Over here," my jailer barked.

I moved over toward him.

"Turn around."

I turned.

"Stick your hands through the bars."

He took a hold on the cuffs and yanked, bringing me up against the bars hard. Holding me there with the bars biting into my forearms, he made a long process of unlocking the cuffs and taking them off me. When my hands were finally freed, I fought off the impulse to rub my arms. I even held my voice level when I was making my request.

"How about a telephone call?" I asked.

There was no answer. The pair of cops who had delivered me to the cell let me have a pair of wolfish grins before they turned and walked away. I reached way down to where I have stored up those words a man uses only occasionally because he's not going to have them blunted by use on any trivial fits of rage. Stringing together a fine assortment of them, I muttered them.

A new voice spoke behind me.

"That," he said, "will be of only minor therapeutic value. To make yourself feel appreciably better you'll need to scream and shout. Muttering releases no tensions."

I liked the voice. I even liked what he said. It sounded rational and I was overcome with a realization of how long it had been since I'd heard anyone say anything rational, all the way back to when I'd first picked up the chick who called herself Lolita.

I turned to look at my cellmate. He was a big guy with what looked like a young face and young muscles, but his hair—as much as I could see of it around the edges of a bloodstained head bandage—was white, and he had a big bush of a beard that was mostly white. His eyes were bloodshot, but apart from that and despite the head bandage, he looked to be in good shape. An old guy well preserved or a young one white before his time, I couldn't tell which.

Otherwise he had one of those ugly faces you have to like. It was tough, kind, and understanding, like the face of an English bulldog. It was also a humorous face but with the humor held in check. I couldn't know whether he wasn't finding things funny or was considering the possibility that I'd be in no mood for being amused.

"They were careful not to say it right out, but short of that they made it plain enough," he said. "They tossed you in here with me even though they've got plenty of empty cells. I'm expected to beat the bejesus out of you."

It was just an observation. I could hear no threat in it, nothing to make the hackles rise.

"But you don't perform as expected?"

He touched his head bandage.

"How do you think I got this?" he asked.

"Performing as expected, but on a guy who was more than you could handle."

He grinned at me.

"That should be my cue to say, 'But you should see the other guy,' except that it's no good, since you've seen the other guy. You've probably seen all the other guys."

"The lugs who brought me in?"

"Some of them. I'm not big time like you. I don't rate the big battalions. For me they don't call out the reserves."

"Clubbed you?"

"Pistol-whipped."

"Do you know what you're in for?"

"Drunk and disorderly. I wrecked a bar."

"You've been told? Or do you just know?"

"Know vaguely, told in detail."

"I don't know even vaguely, and I haven't been told anything."

"Not even your rights?"

"That, yes. Reeled off fast."

My cellmate laughed.

"It's almost worth getting busted to hear him do it," he said, "like a kindergarten kid racing through the pledge of allegiance."

This wasn't telling me anything I didn't know. I backtracked a bit.

"You're expected to beat up on me," I said. "Is that automatic for anyone they toss in here with you? Or did they tell you something that was supposed to turn it on?"

"They told me, but I don't believe it. First thing, I can't see you for the type, and even if you were, so what? I'm no jailhouse Galahad."

"Even if I were *what?*"

"Rapist-murderer."

"Somebody's crazy," I said.

"It figures. They *would* get the wrong guy. You're not Matthew Erridge. You're another guy who happens to drive a Porsche. I could see it coming on, a bad day for Porsche drivers."

I shook my head.

"But I *am* Matthew Erridge," I said.

"You are?"

He paused. I could see he wasn't quite ready to deal with that. He took a temporary bypass on it. Coming over to me, he stuck out his hand.

"I'm Terry Hubbard," he said. "Professional alcoholic."

"Matt Erridge," I said, shaking his hand.

"Nothing to it?" he asked, "or can't remember?"

"Nothing to it," I said. "Do you have any details?"

"What they've told me. This guy checks in at a motel with a girl, but they're not there any time. They go right out again. They go to dinner and all the time he's loving her up like crazy, but then it turns out she's a teaser. They didn't tell me that, but it's the only way I can figure it."

"She eats her dinner and goes off to the john," I said. "She doesn't come back."

"Maybe it isn't the world's oldest trick, Matt, but it's at least as old as restaurants. It did happen like that?"

"Just like that, Terry, except that *she* was loving *me* up—but not when we were alone, only when there were people to see. I didn't know how much of it she was doing for me, and how much for the audience."

There were two bunks in the cell. Terry had been sitting on one of them when they'd brought me in. So I had taken the other. While we were talking, he had come over to sit beside me. Now he rose and walked away from me. He went to the other bunk and lay down on it.

"You know that much," he said, "you must know the rest of it."

There had been this abrupt change in the man. All the warmth had gone out of his voice. He had been interested and sympathetic and concerned. Now all of that was gone. His tone had turned flat and noncommital.

"The rest of it," I said. "I was steamed. I got in my car and drove. I drove a long time and a long way, but only to turn around and drive all the way back to that motel where I'd left my stuff. I had a bottle there and I killed most of it before I fell into bed. I drank alone and I fell into bed alone."

"If you say so."

Terry Hubbard had turned off on me. I could say anything I liked or nothing. He was no longer interested.

"I know it's a dull story," I said, "but that's not *my* fault. I would have liked it to be more interesting."

I waited for him to say something, but he was giving me nothing. I had to ask.

"So much for that one," I said. "She took off, so who was my victim?"

"*You* were the one who took off. Her naked body was found in the bushes behind your motel room. She'd been raped and strangled. They found your card under her body. The maid found her clothes when she swept under the bed."

It was at once unbelievable and too believable. I was thinking about my incomprehensible burglar. That was still past understanding, but now it was beginning to shape toward something. I couldn't make anything of it that wasn't crazy, but it had been like that from the first.

Now I was trying to make something sane out of it. I had a feeling that was telling me that my own sanity depended on doing it, but the picture of Lolita rose up before me and got in the way of any thinking I might have done.

I was remembering her in all her sweetness and all her silliness. I was remembering her NOWHERE sign. It had been easily explainable as a gag designed to catch a man's eye and get her a ride, but now it had become hard to believe that it hadn't meant something more to her. It wasn't only that it had taken her where she had wanted to go. She had set some special store by it. She had gone back into the restaurant parking lot to get it out of the Porsche.

"The poor, sweet, silly little idiot," I said.

My cellmate sat up on his bunk and looked at me long and hard.

"The way they told it to me," he said, "I had some ideas about it. I don't go for any mad-dog-preying-on-the-innocent or monster-in-human-form theories. I was thinking of a girl who got exactly what she wanted. She sucked some poor, silly, big idiot into giving it to her. If people have a death wish, I go for them committing their own suicides, maybe because that's what I'm all about. I don't go for sucking anyone else into it. I don't go for taking anyone else with you."

"Can I tell you the rest of my story, Terry?"

"Do you want to?" he asked. "It's an old, old game the jailers play. They throw a guy in with a sympathetic cellmate. He talks. He confides. He hangs himself."

"A while back you stopped being sympathetic," I said.

He got up off his cot and started walking up and down the length of the cell.

"Look," he said. "You don't have to tell me anything. If talking makes you feel better, then talk. If you want to rehearse your story on me, I'll listen, but you're going to need something a lot better than saying you had nothing against her because she paid for her dinner. That's garbage. Nobody's going to believe that."

"That's not what I said," I protested. "I didn't say I had nothing against her. She teased me up crazy and she ran out on me. I had *that* against her. For a couple of hours there, if I'd caught up with her, I don't know what I mightn't have done to her. Rape would have been the least of it."

"Rape *was* the least of it, Matt."

"But not me. She left me this note."

I fished it out of my pocket and handed it to him. He read it and handed it back.

"Lolita?" he said.

"She said her mother read the book or saw the movie."

"A kook out of a line of kooks?"

"The money," I said, "was two tens. What she ate didn't come to nearly that much."

I went on with it, giving him the complete play-by-play. I had to go back to the beginning to fill him in on the NOWHERE sign.

"No good telling you that you should have taken one look at that sign and run. Do you like them sick?"

"I had nothing on my mind but curiosity."

"That's hard to believe."

"That's the trouble with the truth. It doesn't have to be plausible. The rest of it is a lot harder to believe."

I fed it to him, drinking myself to sleep, waking in time to make that futile dash after the retreating burglar, locking myself out bare-ass naked.

"Since nothing was taken except the two tens she'd given me, I thought it was the kid realizing she was going to need them more than I did and changing her mind about them."

"You went back there because you'd left your bag," Terry reminded me. "What about her? Didn't she have to go back to get her stuff?"

"She had no stuff, unless you're talking about the two tens. She had nothing but what she stood up in except her NOWHERE sign, and she'd taken that out of the car."

"They have some of that," Terry said, "and the rest of it you're giving me can only make it sound worse. They have you coming back to the motel alone. They have the fellow in the motel telling it different."

"How different?"

"You wanted him to get you someone. They run a decent place. They don't do anything of that sort."

"Who's going to believe him?"

"Everybody who isn't going to believe you, Matt."

"What else is he saying?" I asked.

"I don't know beyond what they told me. The next thing he knew, you woke him up and you were prancing around outside with everything on display and a crazy story about a burglar who didn't take anything. He went back to bed, but before he could get back to sleep he heard you zoom out of there. He says he was glad to be rid of you. You had been a headache all along."

"The jerk," I said. "I thought I'd tipped him enough."

III.

Trying to make sense of it, I kept kicking it around with Terry Hubbard. He'd gone off me for a little while there when he thought I was trying to feed him the kind of snow job that would be an insult to anyone's intelligence. Hearing the rest of my story, however, and recognizing that the whole of it was equally incredible, he came around to believing me.

"You offer a choice of two impossibilities," he said. "One is a series of events so screwy that they defy belief. The other is that you could be so dumb that you'd make up a story like that and expect anyone to believe it. Nobody could be that stupid, so it has to be that you're telling the truth. It did happen exactly as you say, or at least this is the way it appeared to you even if it isn't exactly the way it happened."

"What does that mean?" I asked.

Terry shrugged.

"Girl gone," he said, "you took *my* road. I know a lot about what a man can find when he goes that route, stuff like doing all those things you'd never do sober and, because they're things you'd never do sober and you can't face the knowledge that you've done them, you wipe them out. You wake up the next day with no memory of what you did the night before."

"You mean a couple of little things that have just slipped my mind?" I asked. "A couple of trifles like rape and murder?"

"When my memory wipes out on me like that," Terry said, "I remember all the little things. It's the big things I wipe out on."

"But you do know you're drawing a blank," I said. "There's

a stretch of time which you can't remember at all. It's not a stretch you're remembering all wrong."

"And you're drawing no blanks? What about the time you think you were asleep?"

"I *was* asleep."

"That could be a way of explaining a blank to yourself," Terry told me. "For instance, where are you now?"

"I'm here with you in the slammer."

"Yes, but which one? What town are we in?"

"I don't know. I drove till my eyes were closing. Then I pulled in at the first motel. I didn't care where it was. At that point it didn't matter. I just had to get off the road before I fell asleep at the wheel."

"So there's one thing you've wiped out on. You got into your car and drove. You've wiped out on where."

"I haven't wiped out on it. I never knew. I didn't care. I drove west because that's the way I'd been headed, but otherwise it didn't matter. I never noticed because it didn't matter."

"You never noticed," Terry said. "It didn't matter, but you did get yourself out of the state."

"Did I?"

He gave me a town name that meant nothing to me, but when he added the state, it startled me. During my early-morning drive I must, without thinking about it, have been pushing Baby to some wild speeds. I had come farther than I thought. Now that I knew I'd done it, however, it seemed to me that it stood to reason. The mood I'd been in when I took to the road, I had a lot on my mind and all of it frustrating. And frustration sucks a man into feeding gas. It presses the foot down on the gas pedal.

"It makes a difference, Matt. You're not wanted here. You're wanted back there."

"Big deal," I said. "For a guy who wasn't wanted, they were putting out everything they had when they brought me in."

"They're holding you, yes. But you've got yourself a good chunk of delay—extradition and all that."

"You think that's why I drove out of the state?"

"It's what *they* think," Terry said. "What *I* think doesn't matter. I'm not a judge. I'm not a prosecutor, and there's no chance I'll be on your jury. I'm just thinking with *their* heads."

"And thinking with their heads, you're believing that I could have raped her and strangled her and blacked out on it?"

"Thinking with *their* heads," Terry told me, "I'd have to think you did it and you know you did it and you took it on the lam and got yourself away from the scene and across the state line. Thinking you could have done it and blacked out on it, that's thinking with my own head."

"The hell it is," I said. "You've got a better head than that."

"Terry Hubbard, the cerebral souse."

"You're sober now."

"So?"

"Take a good look at what you're thinking. There's the way I remember the night and there's the story the police got from that pimply twerp back at the motel where I checked in with the girl. For the most part his story tallies with mine, doesn't it?"

"All the way except where you say he was pimping, and he says you were asking."

"And that's not particularly relevant," I said.

"Unless," Terry reminded me, "they take it as an index to your character or to his. Once a guy is accused of rape, all of a sudden they won't be giving him the right to even a man's normal yens."

"Let's try to keep to what happened and not what they'll think," I said. "Taking it your way, I wasn't asleep. I was awake and having a busy time, and now I'm drawing a blank on most of what I did. The girl came back. I let her in. In my drunken state I raped her and I killed her. I've been told that drunks aren't very sexy. So there are questions there."

Terry winced.

"Don't ask me," he said. "For me booze is the permanent solution and the permanent substitute. I know nothing about temporary expedients."

"It doesn't matter," I said. "Let's say even falling-down

drunk I could. I rape the kid and I kill her, though there are questions there, too. If she came back, would it have needed to be rape?"

"If all she came back for was that twenty bucks she had a change of mind about."

"It gets screwier and screwier," I said.

"That it does," Terry agreed.

"All right. We'll move ahead. In my drunken befuddlement I do realize that I have to get rid of the body. I forget that the body's naked and that I'm naked. I'm too drunk to notice. I carry the body out and dump it in the bushes. That puts me where we agree I was, locked out of the room with no clothes on, but I am suddenly sober."

"You're right," Terry said, breaking in on me. "It won't work."

He picked it up from me and lined out all the alternative possibilities in detail. Taking it that I was lying and finding myself locked out and locked away from my clothes, I knew exactly what I'd done and how I'd gotten out there in that state and I whipped up a story about a burglar, I'd have to be the world's greatest imbecile to get dressed, pack up, and pull out of there to hit the road and get myself out of the state without thinking to take the girl's clothes away with me and dump them somewhere along the road instead of leaving them in the room to incriminate me.

"Besides, it's too quick a recovery," Terry said. "You're so thoroughly pissed that you don't even think to put pants on and take the key with you when you go to get rid of her body, but then, finding you can't get back into the room, you're suddenly sober enough to make up the burglar story and tell it to the guy with the pimples."

"Not to speak of having moved the chair in preparation for that story," I said. "I'd have to have done that when I was too drunk to know I had no pants on."

Terry shook his head.

"No," he said. "All kinds of ways you could have moved the chair—like you're chasing her around the room. She dodges behind the chair. You come around after her. She moves the chair to keep it between you. It could be something like that, and then, when you need it to back up your story, you cash in on it. Leave the chair out of it. The quick recovery is enough. The sodden life just isn't like that."

He moved on to explore the next alternative. Again Erridge was guilty, but this time he didn't know it. He had blacked out on his drunken acts and had developed a drunken delusion that he'd had a burglar and he was in his locked-out predicament because he had given chase.

"This," he said, "is still hard to believe, but it's not impossible."

"No burglar?" I said. "Then what became of the two tens?"

"You didn't want them. You gave them back to her."

"Before I killed her or after?"

"If you were committing irrational acts," Terry said, "one more or one less."

"Then the two tens would have been in the bushes with the body or under the bed with her clothes," I said. "Were they?"

"Could have been. All I know is what they told me, and none of that was about money."

"How's this?" I said. "She picked up with another guy, and then she changed her mind and she wanted to go back to me. She got him to drive her back to the motel. Maybe they got there and maybe it was before they got there. Either way, he realized that she was running out on him and she was going back to me. She had him teased crazy and he raped her and killed her."

"And to fix you because he's mad over her preferring you to him, he takes the crazy risk of pulling a burglary in reverse? He gets into your room not to take anything but to dump her clothes under the bed. That's just shifting the impossible behavior, Matt, from you to this other guy."

"You're forgetting. He did take something, the two tens."

"Leaving your own bread untouched? There has to be a reason for that. Even if it's a crazy reason, there has to be a reason."

My mind wandered from what he was saying. I was picking up on something else. I interrupted him.

"There's another thing," I said. "There's the girl, the way she played me. She put on the tease only when we were in public, outside the motel room before we got into the car—there were people around then—and in the restaurant with everyone watching. In between, when she was alone with me riding in the car, she had it turned off, but completely."

"That's teaser technique. She works you up but she keeps it to times and places when and where you can't do anything about it."

"That's what I've been thinking, but maybe it's only because I've been looking at it only from the point of view of the way she made me feel. What if I didn't count and she was using me just to tease some other guy?"

"Some guy she saw in the restaurant and decided she wanted to switch to?" Terry asked.

"If it was like that, it wouldn't change anything," I said. "Remember that she began it at the motel as soon as we were out of the room, but only between the room and the car where she had an audience."

"Yes, yes, yes," Terry said. "She hooked him then. He followed you to the restaurant and she went on with it there. That clears up one of the trickiest bits. She played her games with him, but that time she had the wrong guy. He raped her and killed her, but if he was the last man she was seen with, he'd be the prime suspect."

He'd caught it. Our thinking was running down the same groove. Having followed us from the motel, he'd known where to go to find the next-to-the-last man she'd been seen with.

"He brought her body back to dump it where it would point to you," Terry said.

"And that wasn't enough," I added. "If I'm right about her having begun with him back there at the motel just before she got into the car with me, then it would mean that he had a room there, too. The thing would still be too close to him."

"That's it," Terry agreed. "He had to take the risk of the

burglary in reverse if he was going to have any decent hope of switching the suspicion onto you."

"It explains everything but the two tens," I said.

Terry shrugged it off.

"So the guy's a nut," he said. "Maybe it gives him some kind of satisfaction to fix it so that you had nothing from her, not even the twenty bucks."

That seemed too far out.

"Maybe," I suggested, "since he was framing me, he had the crazy idea that I would look as though I had a stronger motive for murder if he could fix it to seem as though she had stuck me for the dinner."

"Either way the guy's a flake," Terry said. "There's no sane way of explaining those two tens. What does need explaining is how he got into your room."

"There's a bolt on the door, but I hadn't bothered with it," I said. "The lock isn't worth a damn. Anybody can get into one of those rooms anytime. You don't need a key."

"You couldn't without a key," Terry reminded me.

"The key was only part of what I was without," I reminded him. "I was without anything. You can't do it with a fingernail. You need a piece of stiff celluloid, or the strong plastic of a credit card will do it. You slip it in between door and doorjamb. It pushes the lock tongue back."

We went on working together, trying to make further sense of what had happened. Working at it, I remembered some further details, but although they filled out the picture a bit, they didn't contribute much.

I remembered sitting in that motel room and sucking on my bottle. I remembered that at some point, when I must have been well along, I wanted more air. I went to the window to open it and saw for the first time that I hadn't shut the venetian blinds. I couldn't remember having been much bothered by the discovery. It hadn't occurred to me that so late in the night there would have been anyone around to look in the window and watch me do my drinking. Even if there had been anyone, I would hardly have cared. I remembered opening the window and snapping the blinds shut before skinning out of the few clothes I'd still had on me. I further remembered switching off the lights and finishing my drinking in the dark.

"If I was being watched," I said, "I could have been seen slugging myself with the booze. Then after I shut the blinds and doused the lights, I had the window open and anyone outside could have been listening to my breathing. I guess maybe there would also have been some snoring for him to hear. He could have made a pretty good judgment on when it would have been safest to go into the room."

That was all right as a bit of clarification in the ways-and-means department, but it still seemed a matter of the man having run too much risk for questionable and insufficient gain. I found no way I could put the thing together to make satisfactory sense, and from the way Terry kept returning to it to chew it over again and again, I could tell that he was no more satisfied with it than I was. He alternated between being manically cheerful about me and being depressed.

He was a sweet drunk and he never did know whether he ought to impress me with the seriousness of my situation and the tenuousness of my story, or if he should devote his efforts to raising the condemned man's spirits.

We didn't have a long time together. I got hungry and, when I spoke of it, Terry told me there wouldn't be anything until breakfast. Suppertime was five o'clock, and Terry had already had it before they dumped me in with him.

"If you want something," he said, "you can get it. It'll cost but you can get it."

He explained that the toughest guard in the place would soften up at sight of a five-dollar bill.

"It establishes a rapport," he said. "Once you have that established, he'll send out to a restaurant down the street and get you anything you want. That's anything from cold fried eggs to a steak that'll give you a lot of chewing for your money. You'll pay more than it costs, but that's the guard's commission, and on the strength of the same five you might even get your phone call."

I showed interest and he yelled for the guard. One came and this was a new one. He didn't look much different from the ones who brought me in, but he was a new face even if out of the same mold. I had the five ready. It worked as predicted. No trouble about calling the restaurant and having something sent over for me. I also asked about a phone call.

The guard showed surprise.

"You ain't made your call yet?" he asked.

"I wasn't given the chance," I said.

"You had ought to've asked," he said.

I refrained from telling him that I had asked and had been ignored. If he was seeing no impediment to my being permitted a call, I wasn't going to risk suggesting to him that there could be such an impediment.

Five bucks bought a man a lot in that place. The guard opened the cell door and showed me the way to the telephone. Of course, he was standing by and he had his club and his gun, but he was doing without the handcuffs or any of the mad-dog treatment.

"It'll be long distance," I said. "New York."

"Makes no difference wherever, if you can pay for it."

I put my call through. I was calling Tom Stevenson's home number. It was well after anybody's office hours and it was just as well, since I didn't have Tom's office number at the tip of my tongue or anywhere the length of it. This was going to be the first time I'd ever been in touch with old Tom in a business way. He doesn't handle contracts or any of that stuff most of us need lawyers for. His is wholly a criminal practice. I know him because Tom and I were boys together and, according to his wife, we may be grown men, but all it needs is for the two of us to get together and our maturity doesn't show.

I got Betty. I had expected I would. I've never called there that I haven't. In his line of work he needs someone to run interference for him. At his office I suppose it would be a secretary. At home it's Betty, good wife, mother of his children, and unremittingly protective of her man.

Before I'd even identified myself, she'd picked me up on my voice.

"Matt," she said. "It's about time."

"What's about time?"

"'What's about time?' he says. It's about time you had advice of counsel."

"Then you know?"

"Of course, I know. I can read. You're headlines, you fool."

"Tom home?"

"Where else? He's been waiting for you to call."

She put Tom on.

"Are you all right?"

That was the first question.

"Apart from being in a silly jam, I'm fine."

"A silly jam," Tom exploded. "You're in trouble, kid. You're in bad trouble."

"At the risk of sounding like your sleaziest client," I told him, "I have to say it. I've been framed."

Tom was in no mood for the lighter touch. He snapped at me.

"Quit clowning and answer questions."

"Ask them."

"Where are you?"

"In jail."

"The last we had here they were looking for you. Five-state alarm and all that melodrama."

"They found me. The arrest was straight out of a bad movie."

"They just took you in?"

"About three hours ago."

"Held you this long without a phone call? Have you been talking, making any statements, answering questions, signing anything?"

"No questions have been asked and nobody's given me a chance to talk. So far I've talked to nobody but my cellmate."

"And you shouldn't have done that. Not a word. Nothing. Not to anyone."

"If I hadn't talked to him, I wouldn't know what this is all about. I wouldn't know what I'm supposed to have done."

"You haven't been told what the charges are against you?"

"Nothing."

"You're suspected of rape and murder."

"That's what my cellmate tells me."

"Where are you? I don't mean in jail. What jail? Where is it?"

Since Terry had filled me in on the geography, I was able to tell him.

He didn't like it but he quickly looked on the bright side and worked at making the best of it.

"West Virginia," he groaned. "You're wanted in Pennsylvania."

"No sweat," I said. "Right next door."

"Fleeing the jurisdiction," he told me. "They can sweat you plenty on that, my lad."

"Nonsense," I said. "Nobody's listened so far, but I'm ready to volunteer to go back."

Tom's reaction to that was immediate and it was emotional.

"You volunteer nothing," he roared. "You say nothing. I'll get you a lawyer and you'll keep your mouth shut till he's been around to see you, and then you open it only to give out with the words he puts into it."

"And a man who's his own lawyer has a fool for a client," I said. "Okay, Tom. This fool still thinks that the best answer to the fleeing-the-jurisdiction nonsense is going back voluntarily the first chance they'll give me."

His voice dripping pained patience, Tom told me that I'd been doing everything wrong, but I'd done it and now there would be nothing for it but to stand mute until I'd had advice of counsel.

"And for God's sake take his advice," he said. "You say nothing except what he tells you to say. Pennsylvania will ask for extradition and West Virginia will send you back, but it'll take a little time and we can use all we get for checking out the facts. That way we'll be in better shape for knowing how we are to plead you."

That was the bright side he had found, and it was all he seemed to have that he could be happy about. I didn't care for it.

"The hell with that," I said. "There's nothing to know. I plead not guilty because that's the way it is."

"What do you know about the way it is?" Tom asked.

"I know what I did and I know what I didn't do."

"You *think* you know. The one thing that's obvious is that you had to be out-of-your-head stoned."

"I drank myself to sleep and I slept. There's no law against that."

Tom decided that his best tactic was to humor me. I caught that in his voice.

"Okay, buster," he said. "*You* know you're innocent and *I* know you're innocent. We know it because you know yourself and because I know you, but you must recognize that you've been making every dumb move a man could make, so now please just sit tight. I'll get someone around to tell you what to do and what to say. Till then you do nothing and you say nothing. After he's talked to you, follow his instructions to the letter. Any other way you're well down the road to hanging yourself."

"Since you said 'hanging,'" I told him, "there's a smell of lynching around here."

"All the more reason for me to get you somebody quick," Tom said. "I'll get things organized and I'll get back to you."

Returned to the cell, I was uncomfortable about Terry.

"Got yourself a lawyer?" he asked.

"New York," I said. "He's getting me somebody local."

He caught the sound of constraint in my voice. He may have been an alcoholic, but I've known teetotalers who weren't half as sharp.

"And he told you that you talk to nobody, and nobody includes me."

"He doesn't know you," I said.

"But he does know the law game. No more talk. Do you play chess?"

"I know the moves."

He fished around under his bunk and came up with a chess set.

"Nobody promised me Eddie Fisher," he said.

We played. It was obvious he was doing it for me. He had me so far outclassed that it couldn't have been of much interest to him. We never finished the game. It was interrupted when they pulled me out to talk to my lawyer, and when I was returned to a cell afterward, it wasn't the same one. For the rest of the time I was there they had me rooming alone. Whether they moved me because they were disappointed in Terry or it was something the lawyer worked, I don't know. It made no difference. Our chess game had been as good as finished. He'd had me floundering two moves short of checkmate.

At first sight I had trouble believing my West Virginia mouthpiece. His name was Clyde McHenry and he looked as though he'd just come off a sandlot somewhere. Even if he hadn't been carrying his first-baseman's mitt in his back pocket, he would have had the look. He had the freckles and the tousled hair and a kid's kind of athletic grace that makes them look awkward indoors. He introduced himself and I spotted the mitt.

"I took you out of a ball game," I said. "It could have waited till the last of the ninth. I wouldn't have been going anyplace."

He told me it wasn't a ball game. He coached a Little League team and when Tom had gotten through to him, practice had already been knocked off by Little Leaguers' bedtime.

"Mr. Stevenson said it couldn't wait at all," he said. "I had to get right over here and shut you up. He suggested that, if necessary, I knock you down and stuff a gag into your mouth."

"That's Tom. You know him?"

He didn't. Just having had a phone call from Tom Stevenson evidently had him feeling that he had been touched by greatness. He explained that Tom had called a lawyer he knew in

Pittsburgh and that the Pittsburgh man had put Tom on to McHenry. I found myself wishing the Pittsburgh guy had come up with someone who might at least have looked grown-up.

"You'll have a hearing first thing tomorrow," he said. "Courts operating as they do, first thing is likely to be about eleven. Till then you talk to nobody. You make no statements. You sign nothing. If anybody puts any pressure on you, assert your right to have counsel present. If there should be any threats, ignore them. They may act tough, but nobody's going to do anything."

"It's been okay since I've been in here," I said. "When they picked me up at the motel, they seemed to be itching for an excuse to shoot me."

McHenry nodded.

"That was the dangerous time," he said. "Since they didn't shoot you, you must have handled it well. Mr. Stevenson says you've been talking to the man they locked you up with. That was a mistake. Talk to no one—and that means no one."

"He's all right, and anyhow, he told me more than I told him. They brought me in without telling me anything."

"For this county that's standard operating procedure. While he's telling you more than you tell him, you're sucked into telling him too much."

"I have nothing to hide."

"Mr. Erridge, till it's the right time to bring it out and in the right place under the right conditions, you have *everything* to hide."

I had my own ideas about that. Ever since my few minutes on the phone with Tom Stevenson I'd been shaping them up. Since I had no doubt about my innocence, I could see no reason for concealing anything. Since the girl had been killed—I had my doubts about the rape part of it, but she had been killed—it followed that someone had killed her.

"If we set up delays," I said, "if we take advantage of all the delays the law allows us, aren't we putting off the time when they'll get going on finding the guy who did it? Are they looking for anyone now? Or are they satisfied since they have me? It seems to me that Tom's set on having me act as though I was guilty. How's that going to help anybody but some guy out there who's the one who killed her?"

"That man's the prosecution's problem, Mr. Erridge. You're *our* problem. I have to be blunt with you. You did everything wrong, sir. Since Mr. Stevenson assures me that you're an intelligent man and I can see you're no fool and you can't have been drunk all the time, it must follow that you can't have been so consistently wrong unless you were innocent. A guilty man would have to be an idiot to make any of the moves you made. What you did do, though, is act exactly as a lot of stupid cops who know nothing about either rapists or murderers think that such people act."

He was a likable kid and bright. It seemed to me that he was going to be a good man one day. Meanwhile, however, I couldn't down the feeling that he was taking a lot on himself.

"You're an old experienced hand at representing rapist-murderers?" I asked.

He grinned at me.

"I tried a mustache," he said, "but it didn't make me look any older. It made me look like I was gotten up for Halloween, so I shaved it off. I'm a hillbilly lawyer, Mr. Erridge, who gives as much time as he can afford to Legal Aid work. It's three years since I was admitted to the bar, and in that time I've defended against more rape charges than a city lawyer is likely to see in a lifetime of practice. In these hills rape is common. Murder is not uncommon, and accusations of rape are epidemic. I didn't set out to be a rape specialist, but there are days when it seems as though it may be all I'll ever get to do."

"Expertise established," I said. "Forgive me for asking."

"If you hadn't asked, you'd be thinking it. There's no way you could be mistaking me for Justice Holmes in his later years."

I believed him, but if I hadn't, he would have soon had me convinced. It was the way he went about his job. He wanted me to tell him my whole story from the time I had first sighted the girl. He listened and he took notes. At no point did he interrupt or comment. In fact, he took the whole thing deadpan, never a visible reaction, never so much as a change of expression.

When I'd finished, I was convinced that I'd given him the whole package, forgetting nothing and omitting nothing. He took only a moment or two for looking over his notes before he began the questions. Every question was to the point, and far more of them than I could have expected drew out of me information I'd been allowing to slip my mind.

At first he concentrated on the restaurant.

"A place with an attendant to park cars," he said, "and a place with a pretty fancy letterhead."

Of course, I had shown him the note. He had read it and he had pocketed it. He was greatly pleased with having it as evidence. The cops had slipped up on that one. They might have taken it away from me.

"If you're thinking it was a pretentious dump," I said, "it was. Not bad, but not anywhere up to its pretentions."

"Places like that often have photographers. Did you notice one?"

I had noticed, but since, if I'd thought of it at all, I'd have assumed it was no more important to my defense than the mesh stockings the waitresses wore, I hadn't thought to mention the chick who crept up on us and popped her flash just when we happened to have been in one of our more unbuttoned moments.

"One of those babes wearing so little more than her camera that she'd make better sense the other side of her lens. She caught us at a moment that could have been great for blackmail, except that I'm not a married man."

"Did you buy it?"

"No. The kid didn't want one. She was traveling light, and I don't collect souvenirs."

"It doesn't matter. She won't have destroyed the film this soon. We can get it."

"We want it?"

"It may be useful."

"As evidence that, with her, rape wouldn't have been necessary?"

McHenry shook his head.

"If she hadn't run out on you," he said.

"Then what do we want it for?"

"A picture can help us with finding out who she was."

"And that can lead to finding out how she came to die?" I said.

"The more we know about her, the better shape we'll be in."

That's one example of the way he operated. When he got on to what I did after I left the restaurant, he had me knocked over with the realization of how good he was at his job. I had been ready to swear that I just jumped into the Porsche and drove without any idea of how far or where. I had just driven for hours and then turned around and driven back to the motel. I was certain that was all I knew and all I could tell him.

He worked at it, beginning with trying to pin down times. I could give him nothing definite on the time I drove away from the restaurant. He was disappointed in that, but he made the best of it. Someone there, the waitress or the car-park attendant, or whoever it was who gave Lolita the paper and the envelope, might come up with an approximation of the time.

I was in better shape on just when I got back to the motel. It had surprised me that the kid in the office had still been there that late when he had all his rooms rented. I had looked at my watch and I remembered.

He questioned me about the roads I'd taken, and under his prodding I was able to reconstruct it. I knew that I'd taken the road away from the restaurant in the direction opposite to the way I'd have needed to go to return directly to the motel. He asked me about turnoffs, and his questions brought to my mind a clear picture of the way I'd driven. It had been straight ahead all the way.

"Fast?" he asked.

"Fast."

"You drive a Porsche?"

"Right."

"You couldn't have been pushing it to top speed all that time without being picked up. How about seventy or seventy-five?"

"It could be."

"I'll get a road map and we'll work it out in the morning," he said. "Meanwhile, that's a lot of driving without stopping for gas."

I'd been telling him that I had just driven, stopping nowhere and talking to no one, and of course I was wrong.

"I did stop for gas," I said. "I'd forgotten that. That's where I made my turn to go back, at the gas station."

"We'll find the gas station. Pump jockeys remember Porsches."

IV.

The rest of my time in that West Virginia lockup was a breeze. They put me in another cell, one that I had all to myself. I did miss Terry. Even though I'd promised McHenry that I wouldn't say another word to anyone about the events of the night before, Terry could still have been good company. There was a world of other topics we could have kicked around like life, liberty, and the pursuit of happiness, on all of which I felt certain Terry would have been an authority. We could have talked.

Otherwise it was a better cell than the one we'd been sharing, and all of a sudden I was being treated with every consideration. I assumed that five bucks went a long way in those West Virginia hills and that it exerted an all-pervasive influence. Sometime later when I got together with Tom, he set me right about that. He told me how he'd gone about finding young McHenry for me. Ordinarily there would have been the established routine for digging up the most competent attorney in an area where Tom had no connections and knew nobody.

"If it had been any other of a million of those little places," Tom explained, "I'd have had no way but to creep up on it. I'd have called people I know in the general area—Pittsburgh, Wheeling. If they couldn't recommend anyone in your neighborhood, they would have called people they knew till we'd zeroed in on someone. Actually, before I called anywhere, the name of the town you'd given me was ringing a bell. I knew I'd never been there or anywhere near it, but suddenly the association clicked in for me. Clyde McHenry—you were in McHenry country."

"You knew him? He gave the impression that you didn't."

"I only knew *of* him," Tom said, "but everything I knew about him was to the good. In law-journal circles that boy is a celebrity. He's made a name for himself in just the one corner of the law that was most important to you in your situation—the rights of the accused. Again and again he's done a great job for those illiterates and dimwits who get pushed around by the law and almost never get a fair trial."

"And to your way of thinking, that described Matt Erridge? Thanks, old buddy."

"That night I wasn't at all sure it didn't, but anyhow, you'd said something about a lynching atmosphere, and you were in the area where Clyde McHenry had locked horns with a brutal police force and a freewheeling prosecutor so often and with such success that they were walking a careful path around Clyde McHenry and his clients. They wouldn't be giving him another chance to cut their legs out from under them. I called a guy I know in Pittsburgh and verified that it was McHenry's town. That was all I needed. I called him."

If I had known and it had worked out that way, I might have had fun watching the guy perform, but there wasn't any of that. Obviously we just rode along on McHenry's past performance. He came around early the next morning armed with road maps and we worked out the route I'd driven. With the maps to stimulate recollection, I was able to mark off for him a stretch of road within which I'd hit the gas station where I refueled Baby and turned around to drive back to the motel.

"Great," he said. "I'll fill Stevenson in on this right away."

"What can he do with it?" I asked.

"He's sending in a private detective. The man will cover the area and pick up whatever he can get for us, but he'll be concentrating on establishing your timetable. We want to find all possible corroboration for your account of your movements and we want to fill in your memory gaps."

"And meanwhile I sit here?"

"Tell me what sort of thing you like to read," he said. "I'll send it over. Meanwhile I have the newspapers. I can leave those with you if you'd like to read about yourself."

The books he sent around were less than an hour in coming, but in the interval I read the papers. They were from towns and cities within a hundred-mile radius, every place big enough to boast a daily rag. They didn't give me anything I hadn't already been told, but they did give me an appallingly clear picture of how Matthew Erridge was looking to the press of three states— West Virginia, Pennsylvania, and Ohio.

I was a fiend. I was a playboy. I was a man of wealth and power who from behind the wheel of his expensive foreign car thought he could get away with anything. There were the news stories, but there were also the editorials. In both Baby figured most prominently. They did report that I was an engineer. Professionally they even gave me a big buildup, but all of that was subordinated to what seemed to be the one telling fact: THE MAN DRIVES A PORSCHE.

Rape, I gathered, if committed by a man in a jalopy, would be considered an understandable minor peccadillo, and murder by the driver of some rattletrap heap might have been attributed to an excess of animal spirits. But THE MAN DRIVES A PORSCHE. The kindest treatment I had came from an editorial writer who called me a throwback to *droit de seignieur*. But any way they looked at me, they fastened on Baby and I came out a malefactor of great wealth.

Around this central theme, of course, there was an embroidery of other touches. That kid in the motel office had supplied the best of those. According to him, I had registered alone, but then I had slipped the babe into the room.

"I know I shouldn't have allowed it," he was quoted as saying. "I should have done something about it, but the man was big and husky and tough, and the way he acted I thought from the first he could be a little crazy."

It was a statement that was hardly designed to do me any good, but I was able to read that much of it for self-defense rather than for malice. If he was going to have to answer for having accepted an inadequate registration, he could have just been using this garbage in an effort to cover himself.

From that point forward, however, he was either out to hang me or, finding himself in the limelight for the first time, he was so enamored of the attention he was drawing that he was going to all lengths to prolong it. He didn't in so many words call me an insatiable sex maniac, but he went a long way toward painting such a picture of me.

I had slipped the girl into the room, but evidently that hadn't been enough for me. When we came out, just going from the room to the car I had put on such an exhibition of unbridled lust as he'd never expected to see in any public place. I had to wonder whether there could be a kid anywhere, but more particularly in the motel business, who had grown up far enough to have pimples without having seen any more than that.

It was the latter part of the night, however, after I returned to the motel, that brought out his gaudiest embellishments. I had been told of the first of those, the switchabout he'd pulled to convert his offer into my request. There again I could detect an element of self-defense. He would get in there with his story before I'd have the first chance to say anything. Then what could I say that anyone would believe?

If my version of that bit might seem in character for a kid like him in a motel office, his version would certainly seem in character for a rapist-killer, and there was no denying that we were in a situation where my character eclipsed his. On our last encounter, when I woke him because I'd locked myself out, he really went to town.

According to his account, I was frantic and wild-eyed. I couldn't recall having been conspicuously calm. I was, after all, in a disturbing position and he had been an exasperatingly long time waking. His final touch, however, was his best effort. Having told him an incredible story of a burglar who entered the room while I slept in it and who had already been on his way out of the room when I woke and who had nevertheless taken nothing, I had, according to him, seen that he wasn't believing me. I had been of such terrifying mien that he'd done his best to dissemble his disbelief, but either I'd detected it or I had known that I couldn't expect anyone to believe that unlikely tale. Having told it to him, I had slipped him a tip to buy his silence. The possibility that the tip could have been for services rendered was not even considered.

The people at the restaurant had also made statements. Theirs were a mixed lot but with nothing that was nearly so anti-Erridge. The one whose story struck me as the most simply factual was the parking-lot kid. He had seen nothing strange in either my behavior or the girl's. In his estimation, we had been like any other couple that drove in for dinner. He remembered us well but chiefly because of the Porsche. After all, he'd been behind her wheel. He had taken her back to the lot and he'd parked her. Then later he'd brought her out of the lot for me. He didn't often have his hands on the likes of Baby. It wasn't something he wouldn't remember.

It seemed to me that the truth of the matter might well have been that he did find us stranger than he had indicated to the reporters. He'd told them about how she had come out alone and had gone back to the car alone, how I had come out considerably later and asked for the car, and how when he brought it to me, even though he had never seen the girl come back from the parking lot, he had not found her waiting in the car and he hadn't seen her anywhere in or around the parking area.

That must have seemed at least a little odd to him, but before he'd talked to any reporters he had evidently heard what the waitress had to say. It could well have seemed to him that her story filled the gaps in his and the whole thing had become a totally unremarkable incident. The police hadn't run these restaurant people down. The restaurant folks had heard the TV news. My name, the Porsche, the broadcast descriptions of the girl and me, had all rung bells for them. They had come forward to volunteer what they knew.

The item that the reporters had evidently found most engaging and that must have struck the police in much the same way was what the newspaper stories referred to as "the girl's disappearance." She had been seen going back to the parking area and had never been seen coming out of there.

It didn't take much reading between the lines, whether in stories or in editorials, to see that the reporters had worked the kid hard on that phase of his story. I could well imagine that the police hadn't let him off any more easily. The girl had gone back to the parking area and had never been seen again. Had Erridge gone back there? Could the kid be certain that he had himself brought the Porsche around while Erridge waited out front? Could he be certain that he wasn't remembering it the way it was customarily handled, even though this particular time it had been done differently? Had Erridge tipped him for the service? How much had Erridge tipped him?

They'd wanted the easy answer. Erridge had gone back to the parking lot, caught up with the girl there, raped her there, murdered her there, and driven out of there with her body locked in the Porsche's trunk.

It was clear that they'd made every effort to make the kid change his story, but the boy had held fast. What the police might have been making of that I had no way of knowing, but I could read what the newspapers were making of it. When they'd asked him about my tip, he'd gone along with the question, but only so far as to tell them that I had tipped him. There he had dug in. How much was no business of theirs.

I saw his point, but I was wondering whether the police had also been asking and whether he had been giving them the same answer. I could have liked him for doing it if he had, but at the same time I was hoping he hadn't. What I'd given him had been a good tip. He had handled Baby with respect and with care. For what he'd done, therefore, it was a good tip, but that didn't make it anything of the dimensions calculated to buy me a lie or even a stretch of discreet silence. But there it was. What I was reading for a stalwart defense of his privacy the papers were hinting might have been concealment of a bribe. Innocent until proved guilty is a great idea, but in practice it doesn't happen all that much. Even for witnesses it can become inoperative.

The waitress was something else again. I could have expected hostility from that quarter. Although I'd been an undemanding patron and I'd tipped her decently, our parting had been something less than friendly. The questioners had found her far more satisfactory than the parking attendant, but even though she had provided them with their juiciest copy, I could detect no malice in it. I could even imagine that she might have been trying to help me and I wished she hadn't tried.

She had watched Lolita's performance and my responses, and she had come to some unflattering conclusions.

"The girl," she was quoted as saying, "she was the sexy one. He was trying, but you could see that it was like that for him. He had to try. He was doing his best, but a woman, she can always tell. It ain't the real thing. The guy is only trying. So a sexy kid like her, it wasn't enough. How could it be?"

She gave it as her considered opinion that I was innocent, but not because she had so high an opinion of my character. It was only because she held such a low opinion of my capacity.

"What call would he have to rape her?" she was quoted as asking. "Their trouble was the other way around. She kept throwing herself at him, but he was—you know what I mean—no catcher. So she got tired of it and she walked out on him, but he had no complaint. She paid him off anyway. Twenty bucks she left for him in an envelope. He's one of them kinds and not even ashamed of it. He showed me the bills and told me right out."

All of that might have been good for my defense, but it was lousy for my self-esteem. If I had just let it go with turning her down, she might have come up with exactly the same estimate of the situation. I could recognize that there was also her self-esteem and this could have been what she needed to believe, but beyond that I couldn't kid myself. I had quite unnecessarily gotten smart with her. For some of what she was telling the world I had to blame myself.

After her, the other restaurant people they interviewed were tame. There was the gal who had been wandering around taking pictures. She hadn't had much to tell them, but she'd had a picture to sell. It was reproduced in every one of the papers McHenry had left with me.

I examined it with interest since I hadn't seen it before. It had even slipped my mind that there had been a photographer until McHenry had nudged me into remembering it. We had been so little interested that when the photographer had come around to sell us a print, we had just waved her away without even looking. I had no memory of doing that, but this was the way the photographer was telling it and I had no reason to dispute it. This one the papers had she would most certainly have shown us. On that one she could have hoped for more than the sale of the print. Married men have been known to pay and pay for all such existing prints and negatives.

The photographer offered no opinion about my guilt or innocence. All she knew was that I had shown no interest in the product of her art. I hadn't cared enough even to look. It seemed to me that it should have been a point in my favor. Certainly a guy who was contemplating crime would hardly have considered leaving an item like that picture along his trail. More than that, a man who had left such an item outstanding against him might well have considered its existence a strong deterrent against criminal activity.

That left the manager. He remembered Lolita. It wasn't often that a patron knocked on his office door and asked if she could have a sheet of notepaper and an envelope.

"I didn't give it a thought," he said. "I figured there's something she forgot to do or something she forgot to tell someone. She wants to write a note."

He said he hadn't taken much notice of the girl, but he also said she hadn't appeared agitated or depressed. It was his impression that she had been happy.

"Elated. Excited and happy. Like pleased with herself."

Those were the words quoted from him. He was also reported as saying that she had not looked frightened or worried and she had not appeared to be in a hurry.

"She looked like she had it made and she knew it. She had

all the time in the world, no reason to hurry. She could take it easy and enjoy herself."

The quote was identical in all the papers and they all ran it. I suppose they felt that it added poignancy to their stories, and it did. I read it and it got to me.

In sum, however, all this stuff the restaurant people were saying came to little or nothing. The crux of the matter lay back at the motel with her body in the bushes behind the room, my card in the dirt under her body, her clothes kicked under the bed in the room, and the clerk's story of our comings and goings and of my crazy carryings-on.

I was itching to get out of there, to go somewhere where I could be asking the questions, but McHenry was with Tom Stevenson all the way. I was not to waive extradition. I was to take full advantage of the law's delays. I was to sit tight while we played for time and Tom's detective asked all the questions for me.

"You let them ship you across the state line and what do you gain?" McHenry said. "Another jail, another cell. It's not even a change of scene. Jails and cells are all pretty much alike. You'll still be locked up."

"Bail?" I asked.

"Hardly likely," McHenry said. "There aren't many judges over there who'll bail a man who's held on a rape charge, and even fewer who'll grant it when the charge is homicide. In addition to that, there is your demonstrated capacity for mobility. You do get around."

"But I will have come back voluntarily."

"That won't impress them. It's not as though you'd come in and given yourself up. You were arrested. You are being held in jail. We can't pretend that you're giving up your liberty."

I didn't like it but I behaved. I did as I was told. McHenry brought me stuff that was better reading than the newspapers and I was sweating it out. I didn't know how long it was likely to be, and neither Tom nor McHenry was making any promises. Then abruptly the following morning, after I had been in just thirty-six hours, it was all over.

Pennsylvania didn't want me. West Virginia didn't want me. The evidence against me had fallen on its face. I was being charged with nothing. I was a free man. McHenry explained it to me.

"We did some of it and the coroner did the rest. The man Stevenson put on it found the gas station where you gassed up and turned around. The man who pumped the gas for you remembered you and he remembered your car. To make it perfect, he knew exactly what time it was when you rolled into his station. He had been about to close for the night. Your pulling in when you did delayed him by a couple of minutes. It was five after one before he could lock up and take off instead of the dot of one. He doesn't like doing overtime, and even a few minutes of it he doesn't forget."

It all added up and McHenry showed me how the sum worked out. The distance was too great and the time was too short for it.

"If they could have you up for speeding without having caught you in the act," McHenry told me, "just on the arithmetic they have the evidence."

That was for the time I'd taken to make it from the restaurant to the gas station. Add to it the time it would have taken if I had driven back to the motel first and then again that additional mileage back past the restaurant, and you came into figures that weren't possible for anything that wasn't airborne. Even Baby couldn't have done it.

"While we were coming up with that," McHenry said, "the coroner was coming up with the post mortem findings. She was killed soon after she left the restaurant. The stomach contents determine that. She had just eaten. If she had lived longer than it would have taken to drive directly back to the motel, digestion would have progressed much further. The timetable makes it impossible for you to have driven back to the motel right after your dinner, and the clerk back there, even though he seems to be no friend of yours, swears that you didn't return until three in the morning. He was up and watching and he insists that he would have seen you. That, of course, could be open to question, but with the evidence of the man at the gas station the whole thing fits too well for anyone to be questioning it."

"I'm not fighting it," I said. "It suits me fine, but just out of curiosity how does that put me so resoundingly in the clear? What says I didn't kill her and ride around with her all those hours, keeping the body locked up in the trunk?"

"Until you thought of the place you could dump it that would point most compellingly to you?"

"Why not? A kook like me?"

"Because post mortem examination says she died where her body was found or, at the most, somewhere nearby."

"How did they know that?"

"Two things nobody can argue about—rigor mortis and cyanosis."

I knew what rigor mortis was. Everybody knows that, but I was vague about cyanosis. McHenry filled me in. When a dead body lies in one position for more than a brief time, gravity takes over on the no-longer-circulating blood and carries it down to the lowest portions of the body, where it shows up as a blue discoloration. If the girl's dead body had been lying in the trunk of the Porsche from the time set by her stomach contents as the time of her death to the time when I returned to the motel and the clerk took himself to bed, the side on which it had been lying would have developed conspicuous cyanosis.

"The underside of the body when they found it," McHenry explained, "did show such conspicuous cyanosis. That would mean it had been lying in that position from the time she was killed until the time when the body was found. That doesn't say she couldn't have been moved."

"But if moved, the body had been arranged in its new location exactly as it had been lying before."

"Right," McHenry said, "and that's hard to do, maybe even impossible. If the previous location had been a car trunk, yours or any other, it would have been totally impossible."

"Why?"

"The body was found stretched out full length on the flat of its back. Cyanosis shows from shoulders to heels, including all points in between."

"Neat," I said, needing no further fill-in. "If there was a previous location, it couldn't have been a car trunk, because no car trunk is big enough to have taken her body stretched full length."

"The only way the body of any grown woman can be stuffed into a car trunk," McHenry said, "is lying on the side with the knees brought up to the chin, and if you'd had her packed in your trunk that way all those hours you were driving between dinner and your return to the motel, at least some degree of rigor would have set in and there would have been no possibility of getting her stretched out flat, not until sometime long after she was found. It wouldn't have been till then that rigor would have worn off."

"So this is it," I said. "I just go off now and forget the whole thing?"

"Not quite. You're not completely out of it, not yet. You've had a change of status. You're no longer a suspect, but you are a witness. Back there in Pennsylvania they'll want your statement. That will be everything you can remember from the time you picked the girl up to the time you were arrested here in West Virginia. They'll also want to know anything you can give them about the girl's past, anything she told you and anything you can bring up out of your own memory that might be a connection with her at some earlier time or with someone who might have been connected with her."

"Nothing like that," I said.

"You may think of something," McHenry told me.

"They can be thinking that," I said. "But Tom Stevenson and you, do you have any notion I've not been leveling with you all the way?"

"It's not impossible that you know something you don't realize that you know."

"Why? Because the prosecutor back there in Pennsylvania would like it that way?"

McHenry grinned.

"He was just doing his job," he said, "and you'll have to admit you left him one hell of a trail."

"Plus all the stuff someone else laid down for me."

"Right, and there should be a reason for all those pluses. Would anybody ever go to all that trouble and so much crazy risk just to do a total stranger dirt? The thought is inescapable. It's someone who had it in for you."

"Not all that inescapable," I argued. "What's to say he wasn't thinking only of himself? I'm available, the perfect candidate for the fall-guy role. If it goes all the way and I'm never cleared, it leaves him safe as churches. Even the way it's gone, it's won him time. By now he should be five states away and the trail gone hopelessly cold."

"Also possible, but the other is too reasonable to be ignored."

"What makes it so reasonable? I'm in a neck of the woods where I'm just passing by. I'm a stranger. Nobody knows me. Back in my home territory it might have been different."

"Back there you have enemies?"

I shrugged.

"I'm not going to say that to know me is to love me, but I've never had any indication that it goes the other way either, like to know me is to hate me. I have friends. I have people who can take me or leave me. There are probably plenty who, give them the choice, would prefer to leave me. But hate me enough so they'd put their neck to all that extra risk just to make sure they were putting it to me and breaking it off? Nobody. Anyhow, as I said before, I was among strangers."

"Even when you picked up the girl?" McHenry said. "That was in New Jersey. Were you already out of home territory there?"

"I was, even there."

"Which means that if it was someone who knew you, he would have picked up your trail by accident or he would have been following you all the way, even before you picked up the girl."

"Exactly," I said, "and that's why I'm telling you it's a lot of garbage."

"You weren't followed?"

"Of course not."

"You thought you might be and you were watching for it?"

"No. I wasn't watching."

"But you think you would have noticed?"

"I don't know. Maybe I would and maybe I wouldn't. The whole idea is so crazy, it's not worth thinking about."

"I could go along with that," McHenry said, "if it weren't that the solid, material evidence is at least as crazy."

He told me I didn't have to go back to the Pennsylvania county where the girl was killed. I could go anywhere I liked as long as I kept myself available to the authorities of the Commonwealth of Pennsylvania. They would consider my convenience. Anyplace I chose to be they would send someone to take my sworn statement.

"And that'll be all they'll be asking of you," McHenry assured me. "In time, of course, if they ever catch up with the guy and your testimony should be needed at the trial, you'll be asked to testify, but there are a lot of ifs attached to that."

"Like if they catch him," I said, "and if it turns out he's someone I know or could even remember seeing."

"Or even if they should want your testimony on what the girl did and said during the time she was with you."

I suppose if anyone had told me I had to go back to the scene of the crime, I would have gone screaming and kicking. Free to go there or not, however, I found myself pulled back there. Curiosity? That was part of it. I had been cleared, but I suppose I wasn't happy about the way it had left me looking.

Perhaps if I'd been in a situation where there was someplace I had to go or even very much wanted to go, I might have continued on my way and tried to put the whole thing out of my mind. I doubt that I could have forgotten it easily because I know I could never have forgotten the girl. She was haunting me and there would have been no place I could have gone where she would not have haunted me. In those hours we'd been together on the road I had come to know her well, while at the same time I didn't know her at all. I couldn't put that sign of hers out of my mind.

NOWHERE?

I couldn't help wondering whether in some way this death or some kind of death hadn't been what she'd been thinking of. It didn't seem to me that she had been suicidal and had taken to the road in a search for someone who would do it to her. It seemed to me that she had been running but knowing all the time that there was something she could never run away from. It might have been something she always had with her, like a masochistic yen for violence and victimization, or more simply it might have been someone from whom she was running, even though she was in some odd way convinced that she would never be able to escape him.

I was inclined to think that it had to be the first way, possibly because I wasn't comfortable with the thought that we'd been followed all that time and I had been so little on the ball that I hadn't at any point noticed it. Then there also was the way she had left me for the man who, I had to believe, killed her. Joy? High anticipation? Smug self-satisfaction? Certainly she had been the loser of losers, but it still seemed as though she had left the restaurant thinking herself a winner. I wondered whether she could have held that feeling to the end. Her destination had been NOWHERE. Had death been a homecoming?

When all this started I had been on my way to keep an appointment. It had never been a matter of any importance. I am an engineer, and at this time I'm telling you about I was between jobs. It happens occasionally, and when it does happen I like to hang loose. In my working time I'm a highly organized character. In leisure I like to drift.

So there was this guy I knew, a colleague and a friend. He wasn't between jobs. He had one going down in South America and he had flown up to St. Louis for just a couple of days of consultation with the money men. He'd called me and, since he'd hit me at a time when I wasn't working and I wasn't tied to anyone by obligations of any kind, we'd had the idea that I'd whip out to St. Louis for the couple of days he was to be there. It wasn't going to be for anything essential, just getting together with a friend to help him with his drinking.

Since those hours I'd spent in the slammer had chewed away too big a piece of time, there wasn't much point in pressing on to St. Louis. Pushing Baby hard every mile of the way and picking up an assortment of Ohio, Indiana, and Illinois speeding tickets, I could have made it there in time to speed out to the airport and see him to his plane south. Tom had called the guy for me to tell him I wasn't going to make it. I called him again to tell him I'd been sprung and I was in the clear. He agreed we'd have to leave it for another time.

So going where the pull drew me, I retraced the road I'd taken. I made myself available to the county prosecutor, answering such of his questions as I could and leaving with him my sworn statement and my assurances that I would be available in the event that I should be needed. His questioning brought no surprises. I had been over all that ground with Clyde McHenry.

So then I had some questions of my own. I took them first to the motel. I didn't go so far as to check in there again. I'd had enough of that one's hospitality, but I dropped by to talk to the clerk.

He was not happy to see me. In fact, as the Porsche pulled up, I saw him dart off into his back room. A woman came out to deal with me. As she came behind the desk, I noticed that she flipped a switch. On a hunch I glanced back over my shoulder. Outside I could see the sign that had been saying VACANCY as I drove in. Now the light had come on. It was reading NO VACANCY.

I tried to work up a reassuring smile for the woman. She was elderly and she was stout, but most of all she was scared.

"If any business comes rolling by," I said, "no need to turn it away. I wasn't planning on staying here."

She left the switch alone. She wasn't going to let me know that I'd made a good guess.

"Then, what can I do for you, sir?"

"You know who I am."

She made a great show of studying my face, but she couldn't bring it off very well, since she was trying to do it without meeting my eyes.

"Should I? I can't remember ever seeing you before."

"My picture," I said. "It was in all the newspapers. I was a celebrity."

"I don't read newspapers. They're all a pack of lies."

"That they are, lady," I said. "This time the lies were about me."

She dismissed that.

"Sticks and stones can break my bones, I always say."

I laughed. I hope it was disarming.

"No broken bones," I said. "You have a clerk here, a young man with skin trouble."

She abandoned all pretense.

"What do you want with him?"

"At least one of those lies the papers printed was *his* lie."

She took a long breath.

"Look, mister," she said. "You were in bad trouble and you got off easy. Don't go making any more trouble now, just go away. It'll only be trouble for you in the end."

"I'm not going to touch him," I said. "I just have a few questions. He's good with questions."

"You read the papers," she said. "He answered all the questions."

"Not *my* questions."

Out of the corner of my eye I caught a flicker of quick movement. I whipped around for a better look. The pimply kid was tearing along the line of cars parked out front. I dove through the office door and took off after him. Before I could reach him, he had leaped on a motorcycle, kicked it to life, and gone roaring out the motel driveway to the road.

I had to double back to where I'd parked Baby. I asked her to give me all she had and we were off after the motorcycle. Out on the road he was nowhere in sight, but this was going to be my fourth time on that stretch of road. I wasn't worried. I remembered that there were no turnoffs from it for the better part of a mile. There was no motorcycle Baby couldn't run down within that distance.

My memory hadn't failed me and the Porsche didn't fail me either. It was only moments before we had him in sight. Then it was virtually no time at all before we were close on his tail and holding it there, uncomfortably and menacingly close.

He took it but not for long. It was less than a minute before he veered off and pulled to a stop. I pulled up alongside him.

"I was only trying to help you," he bleated.

I could have let him know how ready I was to believe that, but I hadn't taken off after him for justice or revenge. I wanted answers and it seemed to me that I might do best with friendly questioning. The way he was, he was afraid to tell the truth. I wanted him turned around to where he would be afraid to lie to me.

"I know that," I said. "So what are you scared of? There are just a couple of things I want to know. You give me the answers and it's no sweat. You make another try at running and I'll sweat the answers out of you."

"What I said about you wanting it and me refusing to get it for you instead of like it was," he babbled, "that was to help you."

"How?"

It wasn't what I'd come to learn from him, but once he'd brought it up, I was curious.

V.

His answer was explicit and his approach was physiological. If he had told the truth of what had passed between us, he was certain that the police would have taken my refusal of what he offered to mean that I hadn't been in the market because I had just spent all my substance in rape and murder. Twisting it about to make me appear in what he called "a more normal light," he had hoped to divert suspicion from me.

"Why did you bring it up at all?" I asked.

It was evidently a question he hadn't anticipated. Under this one he squirmed.

"I didn't know what you was going to say," he answered. "I didn't know you wasn't going to bring it up."

"Turned around the way you had it?"

"What do you care? It helped you."

That was clearly all the answer I'd ever have out of him in that department, and anyhow it wasn't what I had come to ask him. I turned to more important questions.

"When I came back, you had the NO VACANCY sign lit but you still had the office open and you were still up and about like you were waiting and watching for me to come back in. Were you?"

"I wasn't sleepy."

"And once I came back in, you got sleepy?"

"Look. What do you want from me? Nobody stays up all night."

"Nobody stays up most of the night, not without a reason. I want to know if you were in the office waiting and watching all the time."

"All *what* time?"

"Through the evening, through the night, from the time we pulled out to go to dinner till the time I came back in."

"I was in the office."

"Watching all the time?"

"Yeah. I was watching."

"All right. Now, the girl. Did she come back at any time? Did you see her?"

"No. She never came back."

"Not so you could see her."

"Room right next to where I was in the office, I'd have seen her."

"In the bushes back of the room?"

"You can't see back there from the office. You can't see back there from anyplace, not unless you go around back there."

"Okay," I said. "You didn't see her. Once she went off to dinner with me, that was it?"

"That was it."

"Anybody else?"

"Other people—they went out to eat, they came back early and went into their rooms. I had the NO VACANCY sign lit. We were full up. People see the sign, they drive on by. Nobody came."

"Nobody in the room you'd given us?"

"It was your room. I wouldn't let nobody go in there without it was you or her."

"But you were waiting and watching. What for? What were you expecting would happen? What were you watching for? What did you know?"

He tried again to feed me the line about not having been sleepy. If he had been able to get it off convincingly, without squirming and without working at avoiding my eyes, I don't say I would have believed him; but there wouldn't have been much I could have done about it.

"I'm not mad at you," I said, "and there's nothing you can tell me that'll make me mad, but holding out on me, that's different."

I took a grip on his arm. I had no intention of twisting it, but I took a powerful enough hold to give him the message.

"I thought I was going to pick up a few bucks," he said.

It was more a whimper than a statement. It was only barely audible.

"From me?"

"Everybody does it. It's a regular thing in the business. You can make a little extra."

"A man checks in alone. You offer to get him someone. But I didn't check in alone. How did you know I'd be coming back alone or whatever made you think I might? You couldn't have known it. So there was another man in another room and he was alone and you were waiting up for him. When I came in and she wasn't with me, you tried it on me, but I wasn't having any and you gave up on waiting for this other guy. That late you probably figured he was getting it someplace else and you went to bed. So what about this guy? Did he ever come back?"

"There wasn't no other guy," he said. "There was just you. Everybody else, they was couples. They checked in couples and they stayed that way except there was one room it was two women and another it was a woman with a couple of little kids. There was no guy alone except it was you when you came back."

"Okay. Then what did you know? What made you think it was worth your while to wait up for me till I came back?"

"I didn't know nothing."

"Are you going to make me smack the truth out of you?"

"You let me alone."

I turned his arm loose and I stepped away from him.

"The hell with it," I said. "I'll leave it to the cops to sweat it out of you."

I moved toward the Porsche. He came hurrying after me.

"I didn't know nothing," he repeated. "You checked in with her and you're not no Mr. and Mrs. I can see that. You come in for the night. I don't say nothing and I don't do nothing. I'm just there. I'm awake. I'm hanging around. I'm watching. It happens all the time. The guy, he gets to sweating a little. He's worrying or maybe he's only uncomfortable, embarrassed. He slips me something. It happens all the time. Guys they'll be good for the extra twenty or a ten at least."

I had to believe him. That kind of tacit blackmail without any chance of risk was too much this kid's style. It couldn't be anything but the truth. I'd had enough of him, of his look and of his smell. Don't let anyone tell you there isn't a smell. There's the stink of corruption and the stink of fear. I made myself stay with it for just a few more questions.

"When we went out, the girl and I, was anyone watching us?"

"Everybody was watching you."

"Okay. I can see that. We were something to watch. Did anyone follow us? Did any car take off after us?"

"No. Nobody. No car."

He could have been lying. He could also have been too much engrossed with the girl and me to have noticed any other car. Either out of fear or for the profits of blackmail he could have been covering for someone. If he was, there was no way I could break him down. I climbed into the Porsche and I went away from him.

For putting space between him and me the Porsche was great. For putting that nasty little twerp out of my mind I was going to need something more than simple physical space, something perhaps like a drink. I was telling myself to drop it. It was an episode and it was over. If the police ever caught up with anybody and they wanted my testimony, that would be one thing. There was no reason for me to be doing their work for them. All these things I was saying to myself made sense, but even while I was saying them I knew that I wasn't listening.

Baby wasn't listening either. Driving without too much thought to where I might be going, I found that she was taking me to the roadside restaurant—that same one where I'd been with Lolita. It was dinnertime. In those parts where people ate early, it was well on the way to being past dinnertime. I remembered the meal I'd had there. It hadn't been one of the great gustatory experiences of my life, but it had been something on the plus side of edible. Also I was suddenly hungry and the girl was just not taking her proper place in my scheme of things. She wouldn't settle down to being that finished episode.

I pulled into the restaurant driveway. The parking attendant was on duty. Maybe he knew me on sight and maybe it was just Baby. Either way he came on the jump, all enormous smile and big hello. It was genuine and it was warming. It was a welcome change from the hotel clerk.

"Glad to see you," he said. "I knew all along it wasn't you and not because of anything Elaine said. Elaine's full of crap. Everybody knows that."

"Who's Elaine?"

"The waitress, she had your table that night."

It embarrassed him to bring it up but he wanted me to know that he in no way subscribed to Elaine's view of me. I laughed.

"Innocent because I wasn't man enough to rape anybody," I said.

"For Elaine there are just two kinds of guys—guys who make a pass at her and guys who don't. The ones who do are normal. The ones who don't have got to be queer, if they aren't eunuchs."

"Her opinion and not too ill-founded," I said. "At the right time and when he was in the right mood, any man could go for Elaine. For me it was the wrong time and the wrong mood."

"Nobody's going to make Elaine believe there can ever be a wrong time."

"Who's to say she isn't right?" I said. "Most days I'll agree with her."

I was handing him the car keys so he could park Baby for me. With the keys in my hand I began thinking. You hand your wheels over to one of these lads and you give him your car keys. What does he do with the keys? What is the standard parking-lot procedure? I asked the kid.

"The car key," I said, tossing it in my hand. "You take the car out back and you park it. What do you do with the key? Do you keep it with you or do you leave it in the car?"

"I leave it in the car. I have to. If I took them away, I'd be half the night finding which key is for which car. It's perfectly safe. Nobody goes back into the lot but me. I take them back there and I bring them out."

"Okay," I said. "Let's suppose that after you've parked my car for me, I come out and say there's something I want out of the car. I left my cigarettes or something like that. Do you go back and bring the car out just for that? Or do I go back out to the lot and take what I want out of the car?"

He nodded.

"Like *her* that night. She wanted to go back there and I let her."

"Right, and it's a lot full of cars, all sitting back there with their keys in the ignition. What was to stop her from picking one she wanted and driving it out of there?"

"Me," the kid said. "I'm here all the time. I wouldn't let anyone drive off just like that." Even as he was giving me this assurance, however, he began having his own doubts about it. "Now that you're asking," he added, "it could happen. It never has, but I see how it could. I'm right here and a guy's stealing a car. I can try to stop him, but he can ram through fast and not stop. He'd never get far though, because no matter how fast he took it on the driveway, I'd still have time to read the license number and I'd be right on to the cops."

"Another way," I said. "You've got a full lot. Someone's finished dinner and comes out. You go back to get the man his car. It's deep in the lot. She's back there and she's hidden herself away in one of the cars you've just parked, the last one in, right near the exit. While you're trotting deep into the lot for the car that's wanted, she zips out in the car she's swiping and you're not here to see her go. You won't even know you've lost a car till the guy who owns it comes out and wants it."

The kid swallowed hard.

"Yeah," he said, "like that, yeah. It's never happened, but now that you've shown me how it could, I'm going to be worried all the time."

"Sorry," I said, "but forget it. Nothing's a hundred per cent safe."

"And that night," he said, "when I let her go back there, she didn't swipe any car. I know that. I finished out the night and nothing missing."

"I know," I said. "You would have told the police, but she went back there and you never saw her come out. I've been thinking about that."

"Me, too," the kid said. "I figured it was like you were just saying. I never thought of someone swiping a car and getting it out that way, but while I was back there getting someone his car or parking one for somebody, she just walked out and I never saw her go."

"That's one way," I said.

The boy nodded.

"If she's walking, it doesn't even have to be like that. There's no way you can get a car out except past here, but on foot she could have taken off across the meadow and circled around to the road without passing anywhere that I could see her."

"If she's walking," I said, echoing his words. "She's seen a guy she knows. She knows him and she knows the car he's driving; or when she went out to the john, she had a word with him in passing and he told her what to look for. She comes out here and goes back to the parking area. She takes out of my car the one thing she had in it and she goes to his car, curls up on the floor in back and covers herself over with something. He comes out and you go get him his car. You drive her out without ever knowing you've done it."

The kid blinked.

"Gee," he said. "Like that? Was it like that?"

"I don't know. It could have been. I'm thinking it may have been."

"But why? Why wouldn't she just come out with this guy and drive away with him? Why would she care if I saw her?"

"Not you," I said. "Maybe me."

"They were afraid you'd come after them and mess with them if they took any chance at all on your knowing it was him she took off with."

The kid was now thinking along with me.

"Unless there was more to it than that," I said, "and if this was someone she knew and someone she was happy to go off with, then from the way the poor little dope finished up it has to be that there was more to it."

"It would be a guy who came here alone," the kid said.

"And who, as far as you could see, left alone," I added. "She would either have been hidden in the car or she would have been somewhere down the road waiting for him to come by and pick her up there."

A deep scowl creased the kid's forehead. He was working hard at remembering.

"We don't get loners much," he said. "It's mostly couples. Sometimes three or four couples come in a couple of cars. They're a party. If it's just guys, it's mostly a bunch of them together. They come to drink their dinner. Dames, too, we get them in bunches. They play cards and throw all the winnings into a kitty till they have enough to give themselves a party. It's not like we were one of those singles places. Around here it's the bars and the dance halls get that stuff."

"Elaine?" I asked.

"Oh," he said.

"Oh, what?"

"That's where she got her ideas. It wasn't just that you didn't make a pass at her. After the girl left, Elaine propositioned you and you weren't having any."

"So is it only me, or is it only out of pity, or what is she doing in a place where she can't get any action?"

"She likes to dream. She wants it to be romantic, not just business. One day her dream man is going to come in and he's going to be so crazy about the way she serves him the french fries that he'll take her out of here and they'll live happily ever after. She sees herself walking up the aisle all in white and carrying a bouquet of french fries."

"Since you don't often get loners, would you remember one?"

The kid looked troubled.

"Not to describe him or anything like that," he said. "There was a guy that night. Eating alone, he made a kind of a quick dinner. He came in right after you and he left before you. It was after she went back to the parking lot but before you came out. I'm sure of that. I wish I could remember what he looked like."

He was trying and I waited, but nothing came. He shook his head.

"What about his car?"

There was another scowl of concentration and then a slowly spreading smile to wipe the scowl out.

"Yup," he said. "I remember his car. It was a Chrysler and new. It had Z plates."

That was a letdown.

"A rental," I said.

"That's how I came to notice it enough so I can remember," the kid explained. "It struck me funny he should be driving a rented car."

"Why funny? You see them all the time."

Each of us has his specialties, special skills, special little pools of knowledge. This kid had his and it was parking-lot savvy. He knew cars and he knew drivers and he had a sense of which went with which. That one man that night he was now remembering because the man hadn't fitted his categories.

There had been an ease and a flourish about the way the man had brought the Chrysler around the driveway coming in, and again the same ease and flourish about the way he had taken her back out to the road.

"Your once-in-a-while driver can be very good," he said, "but he's never that easy. A guy who drives like that, he's behind the wheel all the time. It was like if you came in here driving a rented car."

"I've done it. You fly someplace and you pick up a rental at the airport to use while you're there."

"Sure, but our nearest airport is Pittsburgh. He rents a car there, it'll have Pennsylvania plates."

The hairs at the back of my neck stood up and threw me signals. "Jersey plates" jumped into my mind and I almost said the words. I just managed to bite them back and put my question in a way that would leave me free of any wondering whether I'd put ideas into his head.

"It didn't?" I said. "What plates were they?"

"New Jersey. It seemed funny he should have come all this way in a rented car, being the kind of driver he is. I noticed it and it had me thinking. That's how come I remember all this or even remember he was here that night at all. I got it figured out. There's two ways it can be."

"Like?"

"An annual rental. There's guys do that instead of owning. They say if you want to be driving the new model every year, renting comes out cheaper than owning."

"One way."

I was waiting to hear his second possibility.

"The other? The guy's from the West Coast or way down South or some far place like that. He flies into Newark Airport and he rents his car there. He's using it to drive all over the Northeast. I thought and thought about it. A thing like that sometimes, it's got you bugged. You can't leave it alone. You've got to work something out that lets you quit thinking about it. That's how I remember."

"There's a third way," I said, "since it was Jersey plates."

The kid's eyes widened.

"Geez," he said.

He was looking at Baby and at the plates she carries. You may be thinking they would be no news to him. He'd seen them when I'd been there before and, if he'd taken no notice of them then, there had been the newspaper reports of the manhunt for Erridge. It had been on the TV and the radio—man driving a Porsche with New Jersey plates number such-and-such. He had just never made the connection. There had been no reason for him to make it.

"She hitched a ride with me. You know that. Everyone knows that by now and it was back there in Jersey."

"Geez," he repeated. "I should have told the cops. I'd been thinking about him but I never connected him with you or her."

"How could you connect it?" I said. "But now how's this?

He knows the girl. He's following her but he doesn't want her to know it until he's ready. She knows him and she knows his car. She'd spot him right off if he followed her in that. That's why a rented car."

"Yeah," the kid said. "And if he was following her to catch up with her and kill her, anybody who might remember a license number would only be remembering a rental number. I ought to tell the cops."

"We'll tell them," I said, "but let's see what I can pick up inside first."

I turned to start inside. He grabbed me by the arm.

"Hey," he said. "Gloria. She'll have a picture of him. She takes everybody."

"Right," I said, "and she does beautiful work. I've seen some of it."

The kid grinned.

"A guy better be with his wife," he said, "or look out."

"I have no wife."

"I know. I read the papers."

I went inside and asked for the manager. Someone went off to get him and I was left standing there and taking on a heavy dose of what it means to be a celebrity. Everything stopped and then raggedly it started up again, but then nothing seemed quite real. Waitresses were waiting tables. The barman was making drinks. Gloria was drifting around with her camera. People were eating, but there was something about the way they were doing all those things that gave me the feeling that they were doing them only when I was looking at them, that I could turn it off—the waiting, the bartending, the picture taking, and the eating—if I just turned away and allowed all these people to stare at Erridge without my seeing them do it.

The manager came leaping toward me, taking in the scene as he came. He grabbed me by the hand and he pumped so hard that it could have been something he was doing for his waistline. He was a young man with thinning hair and a thickening mustache, and his waistline needed a lot done for it, stuff like starvation and situps. You could call that waistline deceptive advertising. The food this bucko managed wasn't all that good.

He welcomed me. He told me he was delighted to see me. He congratulated me on having been cleared of "those ridiculous charges." He said I could never know how much he appreciated my coming back to his restaurant. He called it a gracious act. The words are a direct quote.

"Let's go into my office where we can talk," he said. "You *do* want to talk?"

"I have a couple of things on my mind," I said.

He ushered me into his office and shut the door. He made a big thing about settling me into what he called the "comfy" chair. He asked what I drank and he picked up the phone and called the bar and ordered it sent into the office. He didn't order drinks. He ordered a bottle.

I looked around his office. It wasn't anything special, a small room with the standard office furnishings. Its walls were hung with framed certificates that testified that Wilbur Gates was a member of everything going. I spotted Kiwanis, Rotary, Elks, Lions, Chamber of Commerce, American Legion, and National Rifle Association. I didn't have to guess that the manager was Wilbur Gates. There was a nameplate on his desk. There was also a picture of his fat wife and more fat children than I could readily believe.

"Your family?" I said.

"The missus and the kids," he said.

"Ten? Or am I miscounting?"

"Ten," he said, "and a bun in the oven, but of course you can't see him."

We talked about his family until the whiskey came, and he kept that going while he poured the drinks. It was only after he had poured me a double's double and had shoved it into my fist that he turned to allowing as how his kids were probably not what I'd wanted to talk about.

"I suppose you're wanting to shove Elaine's tray down her throat," he said. "Her trouble is she's got rocks in the head."

"I'd never have guessed rocks," I said. "I would have bet it was nuts."

That should have been much funnier for the way Wilbur laughed at it. He put all of himself into that laugh and it was something to see. For me it gave new meaning to the term "belly laugh." He had the belly for it. He pulled himself together to put in a good word for Elaine.

"You should have seen the way she was happy when the news came through it wasn't you," he said. "It was like it was her they'd let out of jail."

"That's nice," I said. "I was happy too, but none of us can be too happy. That poor kid is dead."

Wilbur put on a suitably funereal face, but he permitted disapproval to temper his sorrow.

"It's a terrible thing. I have daughters, and a thing like that it keeps a man awake nights. It shouldn't ever happen, a thing like that. It shouldn't happen to anyone. It makes no difference that she was asking for it."

"That's it," I said. "How was she asking for it? Did she say something while she was in here, or did she do something that gave you that feeling?"

"Mr. Erridge, a babe jumps from one man to another that quick and that easy, she's asking for it."

"From the man she jumped *to?*" I said. "More likely from the man she jumped *from.* Wasn't that what everyone assumed till the evidence came in to knock it over?"

"Not everybody," he protested. "None of us here thought that. We all believed in you. All along we believed in you."

"Nice of you to say that, but how come? You, for instance, had never even seen me."

"Yes, but I'd seen *her,* and there was everything my people outside there told me about you. You were a gentleman and she was what she was. What's to say she stayed with the new man? Maybe she jumped to somebody else."

"That would have been quick," I said. "She didn't live long after she pulled out of here."

He responded to that with a suitable sigh. Then brightening quickly, he moved to change the subject.

"You'll have dinner with me, Mr. Erridge," he said. "I can have it served in here if you'd rather not go outside."

We had to go round and round about that for a while so I could explain to him that I hadn't gone back there with any thought that they owed me anything.

"This is a crazy thing that happened," I said. "So okay. It's over for me, or it ought to be, but the biggest part of the last day that kid had alive she spent with me. I can't make myself feel out of it. There are things I want to know, things I've got to know. I came here hoping I could learn something."

I was trying to make him understand, but I was going about it badly. Maybe there couldn't have been a better way, one that wouldn't have made him go defensive. If there was any such, I wasn't finding it.

"Mr. Erridge," he said with panic sticking out all over him. "Mr. Erridge, you can't think that anyone here . . ."

I broke in on him to knock that off.

"Contributed in any way to what happened to her?" I said. "No. This started way back and it started far away from here. It was on leaving here that it caught up with her, but that means nothing except that it was here I happened to bring her to eat. It could have been any other place, anyplace I took her. Since it was here, though, this is the place where someone might have seen something or heard something."

"If there was anything anybody knew here, we told the police," he said.

"Right, and anything we can dig out between us we'll tell the police. It could be anyone here, somebody who knows more than he has any idea he knows. Like the kid you have outside, the boy who parks the cars—I've been talking to him. He knew stuff he'd never thought to hook up."

I filled him in on what I'd worked out with the parking attendant, and that did it. He shed all his defensiveness. He was eager to play detective.

"A man alone," he said. "That will be a check for one. We can start by finding out who served him."

Swinging around in his swivel chair, he pulled open a filing cabinet. Then he paused while he was fumbling around in his mind for the date. I fed it to him. I didn't have to reach for it. It had been a big day in the life of Matthew Erridge.

Pulling the dinner checks for that date, he flipped through them rapidly. He was looking at just the one line on each check. It came at the top, readily readable under a quick flipping. It was the line on which the waitress wrote down the number of covers.

The first one-cover check he came on we looked at together. I was ready to tell him that, just on the size of it, that one was unlikely. It clearly said one cover, but the solitary diner had ordered so many courses that there had hardly been enough room on the check to write them all down. The guy in the Jersey rental car wouldn't have had the time to get all that served, much less get half of it eaten. I couldn't hope that my man would have made himself as conspicuous as he must have been if he'd ordered that much, paid for that much, and then walked out leaving most of it uneaten.

I didn't have to say anything. Manager Wilbur Gates knew his regulars. For him that check couldn't have spoken more clearly if it had had the gourmand's name written across it.

"That one's Jess Quincy," he said. "He comes in like that a couple of times a week and he's always got his eating shoes on. He eats like there's no tomorrow. There's nobody but Jess eats like that. Anyhow, it's a low-number check. So this order went in early, at the beginning of our dinner business. This'd be a couple of hours before you got here."

The only other one-cover check Gates turned up was no less revealing. The check number was possible for the right part of the evening, and the character of the order was neatly suited to the man's situation. Line for line it was as well filled as the Quincy check, but with a most significant difference. Here there was only one food item, and that was a quickie. The guy had ordered a cheeseburger, that and a beer and maybe the first of a long succession of coffees.

It couldn't have read more plainly. Not knowing how long the girl and I might be over our meal, the guy had kept himself flexible, ordering the items that would be served up fastest—the cheeseburger and the beer—and then, since we hadn't settled for any quickie, filling in the time by ordering one coffee after another and on and on. The coffees gave him an excuse for hanging around as long as we might be there, but they committed him to nothing.

"That's our man," I said.

Just to make certain, Gates flipped the remainder of the tickets for that day. He didn't have another one-cover check in the lot.

"Yup," he said. "That'll be him. He was at one of Leona's tables."

"I'll take you up on dinner," I said, "if it can be at one of Leona's tables."

"That'll be no problem," he said. "It's past our peak time. This late all the girls have open tables."

He led the way, taking that one-cover check with him. Leona was middle-aged and motherly. On her the wide-mesh stockings were a mistake. Elaine could have been the old dear's wayward daughter. Gates ordered for the two of us, but pausing between items for my approval and consent. He seemed to be on the way toward building a repast that would rival the Jess Quincy meal, but way short of that I called a halt. When Leona went off to place the order, Gates told her to come back as soon as she'd done it. We wanted to talk to her.

I was still the sneaked-look target of every eye in the place, but I caught Elaine's eye and I grinned at her. She worked up a feeble smile before she looked away.

When Leona returned, Gates handed her the one-cover check.

"Remember him?" he asked.

"I serve so many."

"Like him?" Gates said. "We don't get that many singles."

"No restaurant gets many coffee drinkers like that one," I added.

She picked up the check and studied it.

"Yeah, him," she said.

"You do remember him?" Gates said.

"Yeah, I remember him. He's a freak. I remember freaks."

"What kind of a freak?" I asked. "What was special about him? Anything you noticed can be important."

"I noticed he drank coffee like he never wanted to sleep again."

"Yes, that," I said. "We can see that from the check, but what was freakish about him? Was it something in his looks? The way he dressed? Something about the way he acted?"

"All that coffee," she said. "Only a freak drinks that many coffees."

It had of course been too much to expect, but she had called the man a freak. I hadn't let myself hope for anything as easily identifiable as a guy with two heads and a strawberry mark on each chin, but she had given me reason to hope for something, and now she had nothing more than what I already knew.

I tried for a description, but she was no good to me there.

The man's appearance?

"He looked like everybody."

Anything about the way he was dressed?

"He was dressed like everybody."

It was obvious that she had either not noticed or she had forgotten. Having no index to how observant she might be, I couldn't tell whether that meant the guy was completely nondescript or she was poor at noticing and remembering.

"Anything at all you can recall about him besides his coffee drinking?" I persisted.

She looked as though she was working hard at remembering, but nothing came. She went off to bring us our first course. I turned to Gates.

"What about Gloria?" I asked. "Taking pictures, she should be better on people's looks."

I wasn't letting myself think she might have a photograph of the man, but the thought was sitting in my head ready to come up the first minute I would let it surface.

"She'll have his picture," Gates said. "That's better than describing him, a picture. She takes everybody."

"Unless he wouldn't let her," I said, "but that might make her remember him."

Gates had Gloria over and we were both wrong. She didn't take everybody, and our man had done nothing that would have given her any special reason for remembering him. Even without a special reason, however, Gloria had a good memory.

"Single man that night?" she said. "You wouldn't mean Jess Quincy. He's a group all by himself, but I never take him."

"There was this other one that night," Gates told her.

"Yeah, but I didn't take him neither."

"I thought you always took everybody," Gates said.

"Everybody but singles," she said. "Singles almost never buy, and film costs money. Couples and groups I always take. In a group it's usually at least one'll buy; and couples, even if he doesn't want to, the man often buys because he don't want her seeing him looking cheap. Singles, I always *ask* them if they want their picture took."

I was thinking that most of the time there would be no blackmail value in a picture of a man taken alone, but with this guy she had missed a bet. I kept that thought to myself. With everything kept friendly I was getting less than I'd hoped after talking to that kid outside, but hostility wasn't going to get me anything more.

"You asked this guy?"

"He said no. He said he never let anybody take his picture. He said if anybody takes your picture they capture your soul. He was kidding, but he said no."

"Then it wasn't just the quick no?" I asked. "He kidded with you?"

"Just that little bit like I told you."

"Did you notice anything about him that you can remember? Can you describe him?"

"He was handsome," she said. "He was tall. Not freak tall like a basketball player but over six foot, and he had a beautiful build on him, terrific shoulders and no belly and no hips. He had a face like a movie actor, strong and regular. He had beautiful even white teeth, blue eyes, light-brown hair. He was handsome just to look at, but he'd be even better in a picture. That's like it is with movie actors. They're what's called photogenic. I was thinking if he said yes, I'd maybe make an extra print for myself, you know, to put it in the display."

The display to which she referred was a board just inside the restaurant entrance. On it she had tacked up examples of her craft, flattering pictures of beautiful people. I suppose it sucked some customers into thinking she could make them look that good.

The description she had given me was not bad as far as it went. It eliminated short men and puny builds and big bellies and fat asses and brown or black eyes, but it still left a lot of leeway. I wanted every detail I could draw out of her.

"A handsome guy like that," I said. "I suppose he didn't have anything like a scar. You know, some distinguishing mark."

She shut her eyes for a moment. When she spoke, it was with her eyes still shut, as though she might have a picture of the man imprinted on the insides of her eyelids and she was examining it.

"A little mole," she said, "on his left cheek, not one of those ugly black ones or the kind that has hairs growing out of it. It was a little brown one, like a beauty spot."

Leona brought us our first course, oysters on the half shell.

Usually when I am involved with oysters, I allow nothing to divert me from them, but this was just a little too far inland for even the greatest oyster to get there and remain its perfect self, and Leona brought me with the oysters something she had dredged up out of her memory.

"I remembered something about him," she said. "I was out in the kitchen a minute and I came back and he wasn't at the table. I thought for a minute he was gone and he had skipped his check. I started for the door because I thought maybe I could catch him outside. I'd only been a minute and it could be that long before Jimmy could get his car out for him. Going to the door, I passed where you go in for the rest rooms and I saw him in there and I figured it stood to reason after all the coffee he drank, but he was in there just by the door to the Little Boys, not going in or coming out or anything, just standing there."

"Was he alone?" I asked.

"Yeah. Just him, standing there alone. I didn't want to stand there watching him where he could see me. You don't hang around the Little Boys watching the men come in and out, but I was still thinking he could go from there right out the door. So I moved away, but not where I couldn't watch the door. It was a long time before he came out and then he went to the table and asked for his check. He was in a hurry all of a sudden to get the check and he paid it as soon as I brought it to him. But then he stayed at the table and lit a cigarette. He looked like he was going to stay there till he got it all smoked, but after a while he got up and left, with the cigarette hanging out of his mouth."

I excused myself and went to investigate the Little Boys. There was a sign that said REST ROOMS and the arrow pointed to a small hall. At the end of the hall beyond a couple of phone booths were two doors. The one on the left said LITTLE GIRLS. From what Leona was remembering, it was my guess that the grownups met in that little hall between the doors.

When I got back to the table, Wilbur Gates was also remembering something.

"She was in there," he said. "The girl, and it would be just about that time. When she came into the office to give me back my pen after she'd written her note, she told me that the paper towels in the LITTLE GIRLS had run out."

VI.

Gathering up all these bits and pieces, we took them to the office of the local DA. There I had a lesson in why we are a country of good citizens who, however innocent we may be, want to have no truck with the law. I had nothing to add to the statement I'd already sworn to, but here were all these good people—Jimmy and Leona and Gloria and Wilbur—coming in voluntarily with no interest other than doing their duty as citizens, and what happens to them? I was about to say they were treated like criminals, but that would be an exaggeration. I was fresh from having had the criminal treatment. I can define the differences for you.

There were no handcuffs. Nobody was leveling any guns at them. There was no drooling in anticipation of a chance to shoot at them. There was the questioning, however, and maybe grilling is a better word for it. Jimmy and Gloria and Wilbur had made earlier statements. Why, then, had they kept silent about this information? Leona had made no previous statement. Why was she so late in volunteering what she knew? Each in turn tried to explain that they hadn't known that any of this new data could have been in any way connected with the murder. Nobody had questioned them about other patrons. If the thinking of the DA's office and of the police hadn't moved in that direction, how could they, mere amateurs, have been expected to make connections that escaped the trained minds?

They were having a hard time and it bothered me. After all, I had gotten them into this.

"They didn't remember any of this until I started them thinking this way," I said.

Do you think that tempered the hostility of the interrogation? It just opened up a new line.

Were they remembering any of this stuff or was it just ideas I'd been putting into their heads? I tried to deal with it, but I got nowhere. Only one thing came out of it for me. So far as the police and the prosecutor's office were concerned, I was still the prime suspect. Since some inconvenient evidence had turned up to clear me, they'd been forced to turn me loose. I would have thought they might have been glad to have handed to them any line, however thin, that might have led them to where they might nab someone else. I can't say they were going to ignore any such lines of inquiry, but it was obvious to me that their hearts were not in it.

They didn't want to go out and hunt for anyone else. There was Erridge, ready to hand. There was more evidence piled up against him than they had in most cases where they won a conviction. Unfortunately, there was also strong evidence piled up *for* him, but surely no man could look so guilty and still be innocent.

So that effort ended with me apologizing to all those good people for dragging them back into my messy business. I hit the road, promising myself that from here on out I was going to let the great Commonwealth of Pennsylvania stew in its own juice. I headed back home and every inch of the way I was riding with a strangely hollow feeling. I had a special awareness of the empty seat beside me and I couldn't shake it off. That seat just wouldn't drop back into its proper place in the scheme of things. It wouldn't simply be a car seat. It was a void and it was haunted by that girl and her crazy sign.

It was bad all the way, but toward the end, back in my home state, there was a stretch that was the worst. It was that strip where you always see them lined along the road with their backpacks and their bundles and their pets and their guitars and their signs. Riding eastbound I saw another assortment of signs:

NEW YORK
BOSTON
PROVIDENCE

NEW HAVEN

There was one written by a dreamer:

NEW LONDON IF IT CAN'T BE OLD

There was no sign that read NOWHERE, but again and again, as I was driving past and making myself not look at them, off in the corner of my eye I would seem to see her. Cursing myself for a fool, I'd slow down and look. None of them even resembled her, or it may have been that all of them resembled her. What I kept seeing was not her but her silliness and her brave insouciance and her vulnerability.

I went home. It may not have been the best place to go. Home is where Mom lives. Home is also the town that has all those beds Washington slept in. It's a town like other towns. It swings the way most towns swing these days, but it may be a little more hypocritical than most. After all, if you have all those beds Washington slept in and you've been most of two hundred years vaunting the fact, you may not be too prone to talk about what else might be going on in those beds two hundred years after.

I suppose I was an embarrassment to the town. Not to all of it, of course. The guys out at the golf club kept saying: "It could have happened to any of us." And the tennis club gang were saying: "There but for the grace of God go I." But none of them were saying it when their wives were around to hear.

I don't frequent the garden club or the Daughters of the American Revolution, but Mom does garden club. She even dusts off her ancestry on occasion and goes around to the DAR when she's had word that they're about to do something more than usually silly or outrageous. At times like that she comes down with the delusion that she might manage to bring them to their senses.

I have no complaint about the way Mom performed. She was great. How many times she must have been asked the question I don't want to count.

"Of course, my dear, we all knew that he never touched that unfortunate girl. After all, he is an Erridge and Erridges don't do that sort of thing, but whatever was that boy of yours doing outside that common motel with all his clothes off?"

That's the way it is in a town where your folks have lived for many generations. You never get to be just you. As long as you have a parent alive or the people of their generation are still around, you're always that boy of theirs. I'll never know what Mom's answer was, because she'd never admit to me that the question was even asked. I got to wishing they'd ask it of me.

All in all, home wasn't the easy, comfortable place it always had been. Everyone was kind and considerate and civilized, but all that kindness and consideration and civility had to be worked on and there was no way I could miss out on sensing the strain. I took to running out on it, driving into New York day after day.

I could have gone clean away. I'd been offered a job that would have taken me out of the country. I had turned it down because I'd been fresh from finishing a big one and I'd been in a mood for lying fallow for a while. I'd also not much liked the setup, certainly not enough for it to have jerked me out of my yen for a spot of idleness. The job hadn't been filled. They were still trying to find themselves an engineer. Maybe there wasn't anyone who was crazy about the setup. I thought about it once or twice because now I wasn't crazy about being home either.

It had come to look more attractive, but as soon as I gave it any serious thought, I knew I couldn't take it. It would be running away. If that sounds as though I was striking a heroic attitude, I wasn't. I wasn't staying put to face the music. After all, it was all silent music and there's no facing that. It was simply that I knew that running could do me no good. There would still be that feeling of a hollow space always at my side. There could be no running away from that.

Going to the city or coming from it, I always drove that strip where they waited at the roadside with their signs. After a few days of it I stopped going to the city. I was letting the kids with their signs take over.

I never saw another sign that said NOWHERE. ANYWHERE was the nearest that anything came to it, but I didn't look for anything special. I made up rules for myself as though it was a game. I had to pick up the first one I saw, regardless of any considerations. Female or male, clean or grubby, traveling light or heavy-laden, it made no difference. I stopped for the first one I saw.

Some of them I took where they wanted to go. Philadelphia, Wilmington, Baltimore, Washington, Richmond—I took them all the way and then I'd turn around and come back home. On the return I would again follow the rules of the game, picking up the first one I saw. The ones who were making longer journeys I'd offer to take partway. I wouldn't tell them that, but it was any distance I could make with them and then return in a single day's driving. I wasn't checking in to any motel with anyone.

Sometimes it would be a kid who was unaware, never having paid any attention to the news or having forgotten. Most of them, however, did know. Twice I hit kids who took one look and spoke right up, laying it on the line.

"No, thanks, mister. Not with you."

Peculiarly enough, both of them were fellows. Girls always took the ride, some nervously and some with bravado. Not all of them, when they first climbed aboard, knew what they were doing. It wasn't until we were riding along that they clicked on it, but I always knew when the moment came, even if they were silent or if in chattering away they avoided all mention of it.

For the better part of a week it was the way I filled my days, riding the roads with some kid at my side to fill her place. Meanwhile the story was fading out of the news. She remained unidentified. She tallied with no one in the missing-persons files. No fingerprint records anywhere came up with a match to her prints. She had been a dental phenomenon. All her teeth perfect, she had never had a cavity. So canvassing dentists could do no good. Nobody came forward to claim her body. It had come to look as though she had not only been headed for nowhere. She seemed to have come from nowhere.

It was my third or my fourth passenger who was the first to speak of her. It was a girl, but otherwise totally unlike her. She was a pudgy girl with bad skin and greasy hair. She wore jewelry with her jeans and she opened up on it the minute she was in the car.

"What was she like?" she asked.

"Who?"

"You know who. Her."

"Like you."

"How like me? I saw the picture. She wasn't at all my type."

"I thought you must have seen the picture or you wouldn't have known. So you weren't asking about her looks."

"Yeah. Sexy like me?"

"Foolish like you."

"Smart girls don't get anywhere. Men don't go for brains."

"They go for you?"

"You stopped, didn't you?"

"I stopped."

"So?"

"I stopped, I didn't get started."

"No wonder she walked out on you."

"That's right. I'm just transportation."

There were a few others who brought it up, but less crudely. They took the trouble to lead up to it and, when they asked about her, they watched their words.

The next time there was anything like so direct an approach, it came from a boy. I almost passed him up because, even though he was the first I saw that day, he had no sign, nothing but a thumb. When I first spotted him, I debated with myself, I had never come that far in refining the rules. Was it the first one I'd see or the first one with a destination sign?

I decided that I had to stop. Nothing could come closer to NOWHERE than no sign at all. He was a big kid but so young that you could see he was not yet as big as he was going to become the time when he'd have finished growing. You could see it in his hands and feet. They were like the outsized paws a Newfoundland puppy develops as harbingers of what he'll be when he's reached his full growth.

"Where to?" I asked.

"I don't care," he said.

"Anywhere or nowhere?"

"Just riding," he said. "I've never been in a Porsche."

"What were you doing on the road? Passing up everything but Porsches?"

"Everything but sports cars. If it isn't going to be a great ride, I can go with my old man."

"What does he drive?"

"A good dependable family car."

I could hear the quotes he was putting around the words. I wondered whether his old man could be half that pompous.

"He doesn't like sports cars?"

"He says I can have one when I've made the money to pay for it myself, and he hopes by that time I'll have more sense than to want one. That's when he isn't saying I'll never grow up."

"Don't," I said.

"Don't what?"

"Don't grow up. You have more fun this way."

"Where are you going?" the kid asked.

"Anywhere."

"Why?"

"Why not?"

"You don't look like you're having fun," he said.

"I'm not."

"My old man says I ask too many questions. He says I don't have to know everything."

"What you don't know can't hurt you. Does he say that?"

"That and other things."

"What other things?"

I wasn't all that interested in his old man's pearls of wisdom. I was just keeping the talk going. There was something the kid had on his mind and he was trying to work around to a place where he could say it.

"He says I'm always asking questions where there's no good answer except a slap in the mouth."

"And that shuts you up?"

"The slap in the mouth? That doesn't. It's knowing I'm not getting anywhere and I'm not going to get anywhere. It's no good going on and on knocking your head against a stone wall."

I couldn't see how it could be possible, but it was beginning to look as though this kid had thumbed the ride just so he could talk to me for my own good.

"Maybe you don't ask whether it's any good or not," I said. "It's like mountain climbing. Somebody asked a mountain climber once why people wanted to climb Everest. He said, 'Because it's there.' Same thing with stone walls."

"If you don't want to answer," he said, "tell me to shut up. If you don't like my asking, put me out on the road."

I grinned at him.

"No slap in the mouth?" I asked.

He grinned back.

"A good dependable family smack?" he said. "You don't roll that kind of wheels."

"What's your question?"

"Is that why you're doing it?"

"Doing what?"

"Knocking your head against your stone wall."

"Will it mean anything to you if I tell you I haven't been able to find anything else to do with my head? Now *I* have a question. How did you know?"

"You come by here every day, and every day you give some kid a ride. Wherever you take them, you're always back the next day, giving somebody else a hitch. The kids are all talking about it. It's like the only thing you do."

"It could just mean that I like kids and I like driving, and right now I'm having a time when I haven't anything I need to do or that I'd rather do. It could mean no more than that, but it doesn't. How did you know it doesn't? How did you know about the stone wall?"

"I knew Laura," he said.

"If we're talking about the same girl," I said, "she told me her name was Lolita."

"I know. I saw in the papers where you said that."

"Then you also know that the police are trying to identify her and they're getting nowhere."

"Yeah."

"So?"

"Somebody else has got to tell them. *I* can't."

"Why not?"

"Mister, you don't know what it's like being a kid."

"That's silly. You don't get to be a man without going through all the kid stuff first. I was there and I remember."

"My old man, he doesn't remember."

"Then maybe the difference is I'm not anybody's old man. It isn't my job to keep you in line."

"It's what he said about her the first time it came over, about her and you and all on the TV. 'A slut like that,' he said. I can't go telling him I knew her and I can't tell him where I knew her. That would fix me for good. I'd never be let out of the house again. I'd never get a buck again. He'd have me like in jail. With him, when it isn't 'sluts like that,' it's 'places like that.' "

"No reason why you can't tell me," I said.

"You won't say you got it from me?"

"I'll take all the credit for myself."

"It's not only me," he said. "It's the place, too. He'd raise the devil with them for letting me in and for serving me. He'd have their license taken away from them."

"You got to know her in a bar?"

"It's where everybody goes and I look like eighteen. So if it'll be okay when I'm eighteen, why isn't it all right when I'm going on eighteen?"

He didn't look like eighteen to me. He looked as though he had a couple of years ahead of him of what he was calling "going on eighteen." As I'd told him, however, I wasn't his father. It wasn't my job to keep him in line, and I wasn't going to be serving him drinks either. Baby is equipped with everything I want in a car. She has no bar.

"What isn't all right is the people who run that place and all the people who hang out there. They can't all have fathers who'd lock them in the house. None of those people come forward. None of them say anything."

"That's why," the kid said.

"What do you mean by 'That's why'?"

"That's why I thought I could tell you. Nobody wants to get involved. I thought maybe you'd want to."

"She was a fool, kid. Maybe she was too free with herself. I'm not making any judgments about that. She did play some nasty games but I suppose she thought she had to. I think she was wrong about that, but it doesn't matter now. Nothing matters except that she was alive and now she isn't."

The kid nodded.

"It's a place out on Route 9," he said. "It's called Nick's Tavern. She hung out there."

I didn't know the place but he gave me enough road details so that I would have no trouble finding it. I'm no snob but the bars along that stretch of road had never been on my beat. I don't go for the joints where I can't expect to get an honest drink. If they were careless about serving under-age kids, that was no concern of mine. It's the under-age whiskey that puts me off.

"She hung out there," I said. "With anyone in particular? Who were her friends?"

"Nobody," he said, "and everybody. She was always there alone, always when I saw her there. She never came with anyone or left with anyone, not that I saw. She would talk to anybody. It was like she went there because she was alone and lonely and it filled in her time. She was with people, or anyhow she was someplace where people were."

"She wasn't a lush," I said.

"No. She hardly drank at all, but they never hassled her about hanging around so much and not buying all the time. They hassle everybody else, but, come to think of it, never her. They treated her like she was something special. She never acted like she thought she was something special."

"Which way was it?" I asked. "Did they treat her as though she belonged, or were they walking carefully around her?"

The question startled him. He gave it some thought before he answered.

"I never thought," he said. "She was nice. I don't see how anybody could be scared of her, but, now you ask, I think maybe yes. Maybe they're still scared and that's why they haven't been saying anything."

"Laura," I said. "What was the rest of her name?"

"I don't know. The first time I ever was there she came up to me and said, 'I'm Laura. What's your name?' When I told her Bert, she wanted to know was it Rand, Ram, or Her."

"Bertrand, Bertram, or Herbert?"

He laughed.

"I didn't get it right off like that. She had to explain it to me."

I don't know whether he ever gave her more than Bert, but with me he was careful to leave it at that. I could understand his wariness, and I didn't push him any.

"So it was always just Laura and Bert and you never had any more name for her?" I asked.

"Yeah, and she was like that with everybody. I never heard anyone call her anything but Laura."

"Anything else you can tell me about her?"

"She wasn't happy. Somebody was giving her a bad time."

"Anybody you know?"

"No."

"Something you heard or saw?"

"No. It was something she used to say to me. She said it several times."

"Will you feel all right repeating it to me?"

"Oh, it wasn't anything private or like that. It was that she would tell me always to remember to be kind. She would say it was so easy if you only just remembered it. She said people were always forgetting because they didn't stop to think how important it was. She said it was the only thing that was important at all, being kind. I figured she wouldn't be thinking all the time how important it was if it wasn't that someone was being mean to her and she was snowing herself that it wasn't that he wanted to be mean. He was just not remembering to be kind."

"*He?*" I asked. "She said something about a man?"

"No, but it had to be a man if she was that unhappy. She was that kind of a girl."

"Was she married?" I asked.

"She never said."

"Did she have a job? Did she ever give you a hint of what she did when she wasn't hanging around the tavern?"

"No. She never said—except one thing once. I don't know. Maybe it meant she could never find a job. She said there wasn't a thing in the world she knew how to do, not a thing but being kind. She said you'd think there would be somewhere in the world where that could be used but, if there was, she hadn't found it. She said there was just no market."

And that was it. He knew nothing more about her. He had no idea of where she'd lived beyond thinking that it must have been not far from the tavern.

"Not right near," he said. "The people who live right near, you can tell they know each other outside Nick's. She was like me, far enough from home so she wouldn't run into anybody she knew but near enough to come there all the time."

"They didn't know her outside the tavern," I said, thinking aloud, "but they may have known her enough to be afraid of her."

"Just Gus and them, not the customers."

I gathered that "Gus and them" would be the tavern management and employees. I asked, but only to verify that I had it right. He'd called the place Nick's Tavern.

It was called that. There might have been a Nick once, but that would have been before young Bert had started going on eighteen. He had told me all he knew. There was no point in pressing him for more. I changed the subject.

"Do you drive?" I asked.

"Geez. I'm going on eighteen."

"Do you have your license?"

He had.

"On you?"

He produced it. The state lets them drive before it allows them to buy a beer, but that's not the only place where the law has its priorities ass-backward.

"It's time we started back," I said. "Want to take her for a while?"

"Me?"

I don't do that often, and all the time I've owned her it's only been with a few people. I'm not a jealous type, but when it comes to Baby, I'm usually happier if there's nobody's hands on her but my own.

I pulled over and we switched seats. I showed him the things he needed to know about her, things that wouldn't be like what he had known in the good reliable family car. He started her and he slid her into the stream of traffic. He was a good driver, tense at the beginning, but after a bit he loosened up.

"How fast can she go?" he asked.

"With you at the wheel, let's see how slow she can go."

He sighed.

"Yes, sir."

"I'm thinking that if you get a speeding ticket, it'll get to be known that you were with me. If you're right that people were afraid of her, it will be better for you if nobody knows you talked to me. Frightened people are dangerous people."

"Yeah," the kid groaned. "There's my old man, too. He better not know."

"Right, Bert. He'd call me a man like that."

"He has," Bert said. "He does."

VII.

I told him he could drive wherever he liked but suggested that he stay off Route 9, and most particularly that part of it where Nick's Tavern flanked the road. He moved off the road I'd driven him and came back another way. Ordinarily I could guess he would have sought out areas where people who knew him might see him as he rolled along in full command of Baby, but the kid was no fool. He knew that was something he couldn't afford. He was going a route where nobody knew him and where, I think, he was hoping nobody would know me.

When he pulled up and said he had to get home, we were nowhere near Nick's Tavern and obviously no place else within walking range of his father's house. We were near a bus stop and, when I left him and was driving away, I could see him in my rearview mirror. He was waiting for the bus. I took the shortest way to Nick's Tavern.

I hit it during what by managerial proclamation was called the Happy Hour. Happy Hour I was given to understand differed from other hours of operation by a free wedge of pizza given with each drink. I tasted the pizza and failed to see why it was expected to make anybody happy, but I hadn't gone there for the cuisine.

I stood at the bar and worked at looking happy. For a while nobody seemed to be taking any special notice of me, and then a girl looked. After a moment she looked again and quickly looked away. Subsequently she resorted to studying me only through my reflection in the bar mirror. She was with an older woman. Although they were two noisy bar conversations away from me, which put me well out of earshot, when she spoke to her companion it was in a whisper, and that delivered tight against the other babe's ear. I could just as well have heard it. Nothing could have been more plainly the don't-look-now-but routine.

For at least a minute the other woman didn't look anywhere but down into her drink. Then she began sweeping the whole room with her gaze, taking me in as part of her sweep. She could have been one of those panoramic cameras panning across the long front of a posed group.

Returning to her buddy, she fed a whisper into the younger woman's ear. Then they both worked at catching the bartender's eye. He moved down the bar toward them. When he came near them they made a grab at him. They took turns at whispering to him. He made no pretense of not looking. He stared openly. Then he moved to the other end of the bar to stare from another angle. He could have been trying to decide which was my handsomer profile. He was down by some kids who were working on beers.

Bert might well have been among them. They were unmistakably the going-on-eighteen set. Speaking to them, the bartender gestured in my direction. They all turned together, moving as a team, and they looked. Then all together, still as a team, they pulled away from the bar and headed for the door. It looked like a mass flight, but since it was limited to that band of boys, I couldn't see why I should have been the occasion for it.

It wasn't flight. After a few moments they were streaming back in. The bartender looked toward them as they came in the door. They nodded. He turned to the two dames and passed the nod on. It was like something out of a silent movie and the action explained itself. It needed no subtitles. He'd sent the kids out to check the tavern's parking lot and they were back with the news. Yes, there was a Porsche parked out there.

He moved along the bar, heading for me. I don't know what image the word "bartender" evokes for you. If you are visualizing a heavy-bodied friend of man as open-faced as a Danish sandwich, wipe it out. Those buckos didn't go out with the big brewery horses, but for some time now they have been a dwindling tribe. Bartenders seem to come in more sizes, shapes, and temperaments than they used to, but even under modern conditions this guy was one of the more extreme variants.

He was little—nothing as small as a bantamweight but no more than a lightweight, and no look to him that could suggest that he might ever have fought in any division. Anytime he might have had any fighting to do, it would have been with a knife or a gun. He was trying to look tough, but he managed only to look mean.

As he moved toward me, I could see that he was working on his look. I think he was aiming at something like an amiable toughness. Obviously he couldn't get it made. An amiable meanness just isn't possible. He was only robbing his meanness of any pizzazz it might have had. He ended up looking irresolute.

"New around here?" he asked. "I ain't seen you in here before."

"My first time," I said. "I only just today heard about this pizza you hand out."

He reached for my glass.

"The same?" he asked.

It was that kind of place. Keep drinking or get out. I would have expected it even if the kid hadn't told me.

"Not the same," I said. "Bourbon this time."

"What was this if it wasn't Bourbon?"

"*You* tell *me*. You poured it. Since there are ladies present, I have no name for it."

"You don't like it here, brother, there are other bars."

"But no pizza for the Happy Hour. Strain yourself a little this time. Reach for the Virginia Gentleman *bottle*."

Pouring my drink, he made a big thing of it. He'd gone to the far end of the bar to get the bottle and, instead of pouring there and restoring the bottle to its place on the shelf, he carried the bottle all the way back to me, poured the drink right in front of me and then again trudged the length of the bar to return it to the shelf.

The kids he'd sent out to reconnoiter were down there. He

stopped and talked to them for a few moments. He had his back to me, but the kids kept stealing glances in my direction. I picked up my drink and moved along to where the two women who'd first recognized me were leaning against the bar.

"Did you know her?" I asked.

All in a single motion they drew together and pulled away from me. I had them backed against the bar. They didn't have much room for retreat. The younger woman looked to the older woman and the older one shrugged.

"It's an easy question," I said. "Did you know her?"

"Know who?"

The older woman was speaking for the both of them.

"Laura."

"Laura who?"

"Some of the time she called herself Lolita."

"Never heard of her."

"Oh, come on. Maybe you don't read the papers, but you must look at TV."

"Is she on the TV?"

"She *was*. She was raped and killed and for a couple of days her picture was all over the place along with mine. You must have seen it. There's no other way you could have known me."

That was an opening. She grabbed it and gave it the haughty touch.

"We don't know you," she said.

She made it sound as though she had never before spoken to a man without having been formally introduced.

"The name is Erridge and I'd like to buy you a drink."

Again they looked at each other. This time the younger one shrugged.

"Don't mind if we do," the older one said.

She was still acting as spokesperson for both of them. The tone of her acceptance was grudging. If she was putting any effort into being gracious, it wasn't showing.

I threw signals at the bartender. He still had his back to me and he was still talking to the kids. They caught my signal and one of them spoke to him. Up to that point he had been carrying on a monologue. He didn't turn immediately. It seemed to me that he waited till he had finished what he'd been saying. It also could have been that he was prolonging it just to let me know that I was not enjoying most-favored-customer status at the Nick's Tavern Happy Hour.

The kids took off, but the bartender remained as he was until he had seem them out the door. Only then he turned to grant me recognition. He poured the drinks and this time he didn't move off. He stayed with us and made it a foursome.

"You come here often?" I asked the ladies.

"Whenever we're thirsty."

The younger one had found her voice.

"That must be pretty often," I said.

"We're not lushes."

I was thinking she wasn't kidding. Luscious they were not. I didn't say it. I wasn't there to crack wise.

"Just often," I said. "Not all the time."

"Not all the time. That's right."

"She used to be here all the time," I said.

The bartender stuck his oar in.

"Who?" he asked.

"Laura."

I tried it on him. I got the expected result.

"Laura who?"

"This place is getting to be like a nest of owls. All I've been hearing is 'Who?' "

The older woman offered an explanation.

"He's been asking about that girl," she said. "You know. She's the one that hitched a ride from somewhere around here and someplace over in Pennsylvania she got herself raped and murdered. That one."

"Her?" the bartender said. "Her name wasn't Laura. It was Lolita, like the sexy kid in the movie."

"Around here," I told him, "she called herself Laura."

He shook his head.

"You've got the wrong place," he said. "She never hung out here."

"She said this was where she spent all her time."

It was the only way I could see for keeping it going and still protect young Bert.

"A babe, she didn't even know her own name, she was mixed up about where she hung out."

I elaborated on my invention.

"For someone who hung out somewhere else," I said, "she knew this place like it was her home. She described the bar, the booths, the pizza, you."

"So maybe she was in here once," the bartender said. "Who's going to remember if she was in here once?"

"Who remembers anything when there's a reason for forgetting," I said.

"I don't know what you're building, mister."

There was a lot more of it but all the same. These were frightened people and I wasn't finding anything that would open them up. I had gone in there thinking I had no way of taking Bert's information to the police without making trouble for the kid, but now I'd found a way. I could tell the police the story I'd invented for the bartender. I'd have to amend it a little to cover my not having come up with the information sooner. I could say she'd told me about this bar that had been her regular hangout. She'd called it Nick's place, but she'd never said exactly where it was and I'd not asked. I was going to say that when I noticed the Nick's Tavern sign in driving past, it had reminded me and I'd stopped in just on a chance.

I could tell the cops that the place was so exactly as she had described it to me that it had to be the right place, even though the bartender denied ever knowing her and the regular patrons were right in there with him, lying their heads off.

"They knew her there," I was going to say, "and they knew something about her that's making them scared to talk."

I gave up on my questions but I hung in there for a couple more drinks. Since now I was buying for three, the bartender wasn't pushing quite as much. I had switched to thinking about the man Gloria hadn't photographed but whom she'd remembered so well because she'd found him markedly photogenic.

Nick's Tavern might also have been *his* hangout. There was just the chance that he might come in. Among the guys who appeared to be regulars, there were some good-looking ones but none that would fit the description I'd had from Gloria. I saw no one I'd have called an Adonis, but allowing for possible differences in taste, I was looking for a mole on a left cheek. I saw none.

I decided it was a futile quest. Adding what she had told me to what I had from Bert, I concluded that this had been her bar but not her man's. It would probably have been the place she would go when she couldn't be with him. Apart from what I'd hoped I might learn there, Nick's Tavern held no attractions. I pulled away from the bar and started toward the door.

The bartender was watching me every step of the way. I wondered what he was afraid I might do on my way to the door. Toss a bomb into the place as I went out? As soon as I was outside, however, I knew what he had on his mind. It was Baby. She doesn't stand tall but she never sits so close to the ground—never, that is, when she has air in her tires.

I walked around her to make sure. The tires hadn't been slashed but all four valves had been loosened. All four tires were flat. I carry a hand pump in the trunk. I almost never get to use it, but wherever I go, if it is only possible, I like to have Baby with me. When I'm working, the job more often than not is in a part of the world where tires take a beating and it's a long way between service stations.

I took the pump out of the trunk and, going back into the tavern, I had it swinging from my hand. The bartender was watching the door. He'd been waiting for me. He was wearing a self-satisfied smirk. Seeing the pump, he suppressed it, but he couldn't quench the gleam in his eye and he couldn't keep his lips from twitching.

I stopped at the door and talked to him from there.

"There's work for you outside," I said.

"Something eating you, mister?"

"Come out and see."

"I got my bar to mind."

"It'll mind itself or you can turn it over to a friend, if you've got a friend."

"You came here to make trouble and you weren't going to leave without you made it. So now get out and don't come back. We don't need customers like you."

He had his left hand resting on the bar but he was keeping his right down out of sight. I wasn't stopping for any speculation about what he was holding in that right. I walked toward the bar swinging the pump.

"Four flat tires," I said. "Four tires for you to pump up."

"Go to hell."

"Without any air in my tires? All the way to hell on the rims? You can't think I'd do that."

"Who cares what you do?"

I was right up against the bar by then. He started to bring up his right but he telegraphed it. He had been standing in too tight. He had to take a half step back from the bar before he could bring his hand up without giving up his grip on what he had in it. For handling kids or maybe a drunken suburbanite he might have been good enough, but he wasn't up to playing in the big leagues. He knew nothing about positioning himself in preparation for the quick move, and anyhow he wasn't nearly fast enough.

I had the pump swinging from my left hand, keeping my right free. As he started that half step back, I reached in and grabbed, jerking him toward me. Hauling him in, I rammed him hard against the bar. His weapon fell from his hand. From the sound of the crash it made hitting the floor, it had been a bottle, an empty bottle. There was only the sound of glass shattering. There was no splash or gurgle.

"You care," I said. "You care a lot."

I had him bent over the bar, holding him down there with his left arm twisted behind his back.

"What have I got to do with your damn tires?" he snarled. "I been here behind the bar all the time. Everybody seen I been here."

When I'd started this, I hadn't known how the drinkers he

had in the place would feel about him. It could have been that they would come to his assistance and I would have had a half dozen of them on my back. I had been too mad for any such prudent considerations, but now, with him tacitly appealing to them to come forward and bear witness for him, it did come over me that I had them there behind me. I kept the pressure on his arm and I waited for what they might do.

They did nothing. They didn't even speak. Out of the corner of my eye I did see movement, but it wasn't anyone coming in on me. It was a line of people quietly filing out the door. Holding him, I turned and looked over my shoulder. I was bad for business. The place was emptying.

"In case you're waiting for something," I said, "you have no friends. You don't even have any customers. They're all running out on you. So now your bar doesn't need minding. You can get your work done on those tires. I'd like it if I didn't have to break your arm, because then you won't be any good for working the pump. You won't be much good for tending bar either, but that'll be *your* problem."

"Why pick on me? Them kids . . ."

He broke off there. Stupid as he was, he realized that he had begun to say too much.

I picked it up from him.

"Them kids," I said. "They can't do their drinking just anywhere. They have to find a bartender who can't count past ten. He thinks it goes twelve, thirteen, fourteen, eighteen. When they find one who's that stupid, they aren't going to refuse him a small favor like letting the air out of four tires. They do that little thing for him and who knows? He might even stand them a beer."

"It could have been anybody."

"Who said 'them kids,' you or I?"

"You could have done it yourself just to make trouble."

"Not time enough," I said.

"You could have done it before you came in. You could have done it just for an excuse to make trouble."

"If thinking that way will make you feel better when you

pump, you can work at it. So make up your mind. Do you want your arm?"

"All right. I'll put a little air in them for you, enough so you can take it down the road to the Texaco station."

"*I'll* decide how much air," I said.

I let him up and damned if he didn't grab for a bottle. It wasn't because he wanted a drink before he manned the pumps. The grip he took on it would have been no use for pouring. It was a clubbing grip. I slapped it out of his hand. That one didn't just shatter. It splashed as well.

"Damn you," he said.

The words were a whimper. He came out from behind the bar empty-handed. I marched him outside and put him to work. I kept him at it till he had worked up a good sweat. When he began panting, I offered him an alternative.

"You have all four of them to do," I told him. "Of course, if you decide to talk and if I like what you say, I'll take over on the pumping and let you off."

"What the hell do you want?"

"Just straight answers."

"I don't know what you're talking about."

"Laura, who she was, who you're afraid of, what you know that's got you so scared."

"I don't know nothing."

"Okay," I said. "You don't want to use your head. Go on pumping and put your back into it."

I kept him on the first tire only until he had it up to where I could roll on it for the short distance to the nearest filling station.

"For now," I said, "that'll be enough on that one. Get on to the second. When you have all four up that far and you still know nothing, you'll go back around and bring the four of them all the way up. That's going to be a lot of pumping."

"Why do you come asking me?" he wailed. "Why don't you go ask her old man?"

"You talk or you pump, but you've got to say something useful. Who's her old man and where do I find him?"

"His name's Hofstetter, Lou Hofstetter. You can find him in the phone book. It's Ludwig Hofstetter in the book."

By wrapping too many words around the little he was saying he might have been hoping to make it seem as though he were saying enough. It did him no good. I wasn't counting words. I wanted some meat.

"Keep going," I said.

He thought I was talking about the pumping.

"That's what you wanted to know, ain't it?"

"It's a beginning. Is he scared too?"

"I don't know what he is except he's a son of a bitch. You go ask him."

"But you know what *you're* scared of."

"I ain't scared of nothing."

"The police are looking for an identification. You could have given them one and you haven't. Inside you were scared shitless for fear someone would tell me something, but nobody did. Everyone's scared."

"What's to be scared of?"

I shoved him back to the pump.

"Go on with the tires," I said, "and don't stop till you're ready to give me something I want to hear."

"How should I know what crazy thing you want?"

"If you don't know, you have your suspicions. Keep pumping. You can listen while you sweat. You were making sure nobody told me anything and you sent the kids out to work on my tires. What was that for?"

"It was so you wouldn't come back here. You'd go to bars where you don't have trouble with your car."

"So that didn't work," I said. "*I* don't have trouble. *You* do. Since you scare easy, you're going to have to learn to be scared of me."

"I ain't scared of nobody. I ain't behind that bar for my health. I got to do business. You hang around, you're bad for business."

"Why?"

"People, they come to a pub to get cheered up. They don't

come to get depressed. People see you, they know you. You remind them of her and what happened to her and how it happened. That's depressing, and for the gals it's worse. It can scare them away. Sure, they turned you loose. They can't prove it on you, but maybe that don't mean nothing."

"There's an easier way to get rid of me and it's one that'll work."

"How?"

I wasn't bothering to answer that question.

"Get on with the pumping," I said. "It'll come to you."

"I told you everything I know."

"You haven't told me why everybody's clammed up."

He worked at telling me. Speaking for himself and for the people who knew her from seeing her at the tavern, he said, they knew nothing. Having so little to volunteer, they had volunteered nothing because they didn't have enough to give to make it seem worthwhile to get involved with the police.

"If you know nothing more than you say, how could you get involved?"

"The cops are just going to take what I tell them without they work me over for anything more?" he said. "Mister, you got to be kidding. Look the way I got you on my back."

There was some reason in that but not nearly enough.

"If you let the air out of a police car's tires . . ." I said.

"Honest. I don't know nothing."

"She had a husband."

"You know more about her than I do. I never knew that."

"You thought they were just shacked up?"

"Who?"

"Laura and the guy."

"I never seen no guy."

"Maybe not, but you know about him. He's got you scared."

"Look. I know she's got her old man. I know he's a crazy bastard. He's keeping his trap shut. He ain't claiming his daughter's body or anything. What's that for? He's her old man. If he ain't saying nothing, who's to talk? I need a mean son of a bitch like that teeing off on me?"

"Ten-dollar bills mean anything to you?"

"They don't buy what you used to get for a five."

"Anything you can do with them that's not spending them?" I asked.

"Put them in the bank and save them. Sock them away in a teapot on the kitchen shelf. The way things is going, it'll come a time when you can light cigars with them."

I hadn't been asking for a lecture on inflation and it could have been that he'd launched into that in an effort to evade answering, but it was my feeling that on this item he was telling the truth, covering up nothing, putting on no pretense of ignorance. I believed he didn't know anything about the two tens.

The guy was an assiduous and even an accomplished liar, but he was too frightened to keep it under proper control. Each time I came at him with a question he was afraid to answer, his panic showed. On my questions about the tens, he showed nothing but curiosity.

I had to recognize that he had given me all he would ever dare to give me. He was in a sweat of despair over having told me even the little he'd let me have. I booted him in the ass and took the pump away from him.

"Go back to your bar," I said, "and pray that there is a Ludwig Hofstetter and that he is her father."

"Go see him," the bartender said. He scurried to the door of his tavern and from that distance he tried for the last word. "You'll go together good, him and you."

I knew it was meant for an insult. I hoped I could take it for a prophecy. I worked at each of the tires in turn, bringing them all up to where I could manage a slow-driven, squishy couple of hundred yards.

That was enough to take me to a gas station where I gave proper attention to Baby's needs and I also had a look at a phone book. That was easy. There was only one Hofstetter and he was a Ludwig. The address was a couple of towns away. If you don't know the northeastern states, that might seem like a long distance. It isn't. In northern New Jersey each town elbows the next one with no open country between. It was no more than half an hour's drive from Nick's Tavern, and I'm not talking about anything like Baby's top speed. To take much longer for it, you'd have to use an oxcart.

Measured socially, however, it was worlds away. Since, among other things, that part of Jersey is one of New York City's major gateways to the West, it is sliced every which way by highways and parkways. In this huddle of towns the highways have taken over the social function once performed by the railroad tracks. What used to be the wrong side of the tracks is now the wrong side of the highway. The highway itself, of course, is always wrong.

Going from the tavern to the Hofstetter address took you across, first, an upper-middle area, then a highway, and beyond the highway a lower-middle section. After another highway a stretch of upper-upper was terminated by a third highway, with Hofstetter beyond in an area that ran from lower-middle to blue-collar.

People who lived down there would do their drinking in a bar along one of the highways that formed the boundaries of their district. To range farther from home they would go along one of their highways down there. They wouldn't go across highway after highway to hit a joint on Route 9 that was indistinguishable from any of the dumps nearer home. They wouldn't, that is, unless they were looking for a pub where the style suited them but where at the same time nobody would know them.

As I was driving down to that Hofstetter address, it became obvious to me that during the time she had been frequenting Nick's Tavern the girl could hardly have been living in her father's house. It was far too long a walk. There was no bus route that came within miles of connecting the two places. Doing it would have been all but impossible.

She would have been going against the traffic all the way. I'm not saying that nobody ever drove from the one area to the other, but to make a regular and frequent thing of thumbing a ride back and forth over a single route you can't stand around waiting for the occasional oddity who might be going your way. You have to go with the flow of the traffic.

There was only one reasonable way she could have made the journey, and that was by car. Bert had been explicit about that. She didn't drive over to Nick's. She never had a car parked outside the tavern. He had never seen anyone deliver her to the place or come by to pick her up. It had been his impression that she, like himself, came and went on foot.

She had, of course, told me that she was married and that the guy had run out on her. I was telling myself that it didn't necessarily follow that she had gone home to Daddy. Actually, I knew the destination she had chosen for herself: NOWHERE. Even if I were to assume, therefore, that she had gone home to her father, it would have been only temporarily before she had taken to the road. All I had was that she had hung out at Nick's. Nobody had said she'd been there during the last day or two of her life.

The street, when I came to it, was like a million other streets. It was lined with two-story stucco houses that had begun as an endless succession of identical twins. Since they were long years away from being new houses, use, accident, and—in a few—some measure of individual taste had established differences. One might have a baby's stroller by its front steps, another a bicycle, and a third a wheelchair. They all had lawns, and they ranged from shaggy and weed-grown to a putting-green perfection. Most of the lawns were punctuated with the standard shrubs, and many were inhabited by pottery rabbits, squirrels, and ducks, plus an occasional pottery leprechaun.

The Hofstetter house was a standout. In the whole area—on a guess I am willing to answer for even those parts of it I've never seen—there couldn't have been another like it. Its lawn was an immaculate stretch of green velvet. There were none of the standard shrubs. In their place were roses and such roses as would make any garden-club lady go home and eat bug killer. The house itself was visible only as a shape over which climbing plants grew.

Nothing showed but roof, chimney, door, and windows. The rest was a solid matting of leaf and blossom—wisteria here, rambling roses there, ivy the rest of the way.

Beautiful?

Hardly.

There was too much of it. Take it item by item and you could see it as the product of masterly gardening. Take it all in all and it had a sinister, jungle look. All those vines with their ropy, avid tendrils weren't ornamenting the house, they were smothering it.

I parked Baby out front and walked up a path between the roses. In all their splendor there was something about them that seemed hostile. They grew too close to the path. It was no delusion that their thorns reached for me as I threaded my way between the bushes. I was not at all certain that they had been planted there for ornament. They could have been a way of keeping the world at a distance.

I looked for a doorbell. If there was one, you could find it only by taking a machete to the wisteria and hacking your way into it. I had no machete and no hope that my pocketknife would be adequate. I knocked. The door opened so immediately on my knock that it may have been snatched away to prevent my profaning it with another knuckle.

A man stood in the doorway and looked me over. It was my first thought that this would be an older brother. The family resemblance was strong, but what in the girl had been gentle and vulnerable was hard and brutish in the man.

He was wearing dark work pants and a white undershirt and he was barefoot. He wasn't a big guy but he had the build of a professional strong man. All over his bare arms and shoulders the muscles jumped out at you, each one differentiated, each one asserting itself individually. This was a guy who had to be hooked on the body-building deal. Nobody gets that way without working at it.

Although it was my first thought that he was too young to be the girl's father, second thoughts amended that. She had been young, very young, and this guy was in his late thirties or early forties, easily within the biological possibilities.

"I don't want any," he said and moved to shut the door in my face.

I stood my ground.

"I'm not selling any," I said.

For a moment it looked as though the door was going to come at me and feed me my nose, but he pulled back on it and just stood there waiting for me to speak my piece.

VIII.

I had no way of determining whether there would be a reception of this sort for anyone who came to that door or whether the hostility and suspicion arose from his knowing who I was. The bartender back at the tavern could easily have phoned an alert, but it was hardly likely that Ludwig Hofstetter, even without forewarning, wouldn't have recognized me on sight.

Kids thumbing along the road had picked up on me and on the Porsche. In the tavern I had been recognized even without Baby. When the kids had gone out to look at the car, it had been only for verification. Now Hofstetter had all of it right in front of him—me and, sufficiently visible past his roses, Baby. If it had been so easy for all those people, it could hardly have been difficult for her father.

"My name's Erridge, Mr. Hofstetter, Matt Erridge. May I come in?"

"What for?"

"So we can talk."

"What we got to talk about?"

"Your daughter."

"I got no daughter."

"I know, but you had a daughter, Laura."

"Don't you go telling me what I had, mister."

If it hadn't been for that unmistakable family resemblance I could have believed the man, assuming that the bartender, in the mistaken notion that it would get me off his back, had sent me off on a wild-goose chase.

"She was with me for a good piece of her last day alive."

"You can go boast about that to somebody else. You'll maybe find somebody who'll be interested."

"You're *not?*"

"It's no skin off my ass."

"What about the man who killed her? You want him to get away with it?"

"She had it coming. The wages of sin are death."

"Just her?" I asked. "The man doesn't get to collect his wages?"

"You want to pay him off, that's your business. Don't come around bugging me with it."

"You don't even want to help?"

"It's no skin off my ass."

This seemed to be a guy who valued nothing but the skin on his ass.

"The police have been trying to sweat out an identification. She's lying in a Pennsylvania morgue unclaimed. You think they're going to like your not coming forward?"

"So they won't like it. They don't have to have everything the way they like it. What are they going to do about it? Not give me the community award for good citizenship?"

"And you don't care what happens to her body?"

"Why?" he asked. "They have no garbage collection out there in Pennsylvania?"

"Your flesh and blood, Mr. Hofstetter."

"My shit, Mr. Erridge."

"I liked her," I said. "She was mixed up and silly and unhappy, but she had courage and imagination and she was young. Kids don't have death coming to them, no matter what."

"You liked her, so now you want to suck me into paying for her funeral. Screw that. You liked her. You get her buried. You with your fancy automobile, you're loaded. If there's no room in your family plot for putting away your whores, you can buy one of them mausoleums. Don't bother me with it."

"Ten-dollar bills," I said.

"Not one red cent."

"I'm not asking you for anything. I just want to know what they mean."

"They mean she was selling herself cheap," her father said.

"Special ten-dollar bills," I persisted. "They were two bills that meant something that other tens didn't mean. Other tens might just be money. These were special."

"I know a guy who owns a bar," Hofstetter said. "He's got a one-dollar bill in a frame and it's hanging behind the bar. It's the first buck he took in when he opened the place. Two tens could be what she got for her first lay, or isn't that the going price? You're in the market. You should know."

All the time he stood framed in the doorway he kept rippling the muscles, bringing up first one set and then another. He might have been flashing me messages but it just didn't strike me that way. It seemed more like a nonstop performance, flexing and unflexing, doing a tension-relaxation tour of his whole body. The guy was a sinewy Narcissus, so much in love with his own muscle structure that it didn't seem possible that he could ever have had time for anything else. I wondered about the roses. They took tending and care. They showed no signs of neglect, not even of any short-term, recent neglect.

"Who does the great roses?" I asked.

I was thinking a show of interest in one of the man's passions might soften him up a bit. I couldn't very well ask him who does the great muscles. What I'd hoped would sound like a friendly query, however, didn't go down that way with him.

"Flowers for the funeral?" he said. "No way."

"I'd like to take care of that," I told him.

"That's *your* business. Don't come bothering me with it."

"They'd never turn her body over to me," I said. "I'm no relative. I'm nothing, just a guy who gave her a lift. If you just come forward and claim the body, I'll take it off your hands and it won't cost you anything, not even a thorn off your roses."

"She's nothing to me."

"You won't even do that much?"

"You can bury her. Maybe I'll come spit on her grave."

"What about her husband?"

"Who's he?"

"I'm asking *you*," I said.

"You've got to be kidding. Nobody marries the likes of her."

"But she was married."

"Don't make me laugh."

"All right," I said. "Maybe they weren't married. Maybe they were just shacking up. It makes no difference. Who was he?"

"It makes a difference."

"If you say so, but who was he?"

"Don't ask me. I didn't keep tabs."

"Maybe if you'd kept tabs, you'd have found out she wasn't what you think."

"You think what you think," he said. "I know what I think."

"A very handsome guy, like a movie actor, and with a little mole on his left cheek?"

"What about him?"

"Who is he?"

"How would I know?"

"Then you won't tell me anything? You may have to tell the police."

"I don't have to do anything. For you maybe she died that night. For me she never lived. Anything else you want to know?"

"Yes," I said. "Just one thing more. What are the muscles for?"

I thought he might try to show me. I wanted him to. That body-beautiful crap is just to look at. It isn't to use. I was waiting for him to swing on me. I wanted to knock him on his ass where he had all that skin he set so much store by. I could think of no more satisfying way to end the visit.

He didn't show me. He told me the whole crazy harangue. It was eating right and living right. It was clean living. No smoking. No drinking. No screwing. He had a clean body, he said, and—so help me—clean thoughts.

It was too much.

"The thoughts you have about her? You call those clean? Brother, you've got the world's sewer for a mind."

"I have no thoughts about her," he said. "She doesn't exist. You don't exist."

It was no use hanging around for any more of that. I told him goodnight. I even thanked him for giving me his time. He said nothing. He just stood there holding the door, and the way he held it was saying he was only waiting for me to step out of the way so he could shut it. I pulled out of there. Whether he was putting on a big act or he was the nut he seemed to be, I was getting nowhere with him.

Driving home, I added up what I had accomplished through all my efforts that day. It came to a sum that was so close to nothing as made no difference. It seemed obvious that this detecting bit wasn't my game. I was ready to turn it over to the pros and make a try at forgetting it.

The first thing I did on coming into the house was to put a call through to that DA out in western Pennsylvania. I filled him in on what I had learned. He came up with a reaction I hadn't expected.

"Think he killed her?" he asked.

"Her father?"

"He sounds like a religious nut," the guy said. "Around here we get them back in the mountains, and to the east of us in the Pennsylvania Dutch country it's even worse. You hear that 'wages of sin' junk and look out, brother. Somebody comes up with the idea that he's the hand of the Lord."

"What about the beautiful man with the mole on his cheek?" I asked.

"Couldn't have been her old man?"

The question set me back on my heels. It opened new vistas. She came all over happy and self-satisfied at what she thought was a chance to go home to Daddy and she walked out on me for it? Incest? Then, there was that crazy business of the two tens. He wouldn't steal. The hand of the Lord doesn't pick pockets, but what about retrieving what he thinks is his own? The picture had a peculiar rightness to it. I could figure the guy for being at once miserly and scrupulous. What was hers was his, and none of it was going to get away from him. He could steal it back and that wouldn't be stealing, but he wouldn't take even a button of mine.

I was almost persuaded but I pulled away from thinking it. Maybe because I didn't want to I found something to grab at.

"Not tall enough," I said, "and no mole on his left cheek."

"Yes," he said but with no conviction. "All the same, we'll fix it to have him watched and checked out. Thanks for the help."

I came away from the phone telling myself that the prosecutor was out of his skull. He was so suspect-hungry that he was crazy with it. First he had grabbed at me. I was remembering the way he'd reacted when the evidence forced him to give up on me. The evidence was there. He couldn't hold me, but he wasn't going to believe that there was no trick in it. In his head I'd been guilty even when proved innocent.

Now he'd jumped at the idea that her heart belonged to Daddy. Daddy was a couple of inches too short and there was no mole on his left cheek, but it was the mixture as before. If the evidence didn't fit, he wasn't about to believe the evidence. There had to be a trick to it somewhere. I asked myself what the guy could be thinking. Elevator shoes? Could a mole that looked like a beauty spot have been a beauty spot fixed to look like a mole?

Descriptions always ask for identifying marks. Why not manufacture an identifying mark to louse the description up? The more I thought about it, the better I understood that DA. Try hard enough and you'll find a way to persuade yourself of anything.

There was just one thing I couldn't find a way of going with, and that was the incest bit. I wanted to put it out of my head, but in spite of myself I kept working at it. The kid had grown up and she had been a bad girl. She had strayed from the path of virtue? Of innocence? Of virginity? She had sinned. I was trying to think about it in what might have been Ludwig Hofstetter's words. He'd kicked her out of the house. "You're no daughter of mine any more. Go and never darken my door again."

I knew I was reaching back a century for the words if not for the sentiment, but I had no idea of what the modern words for such a situation would be. I seriously doubted that there would have been any modern words for it.

Whatever the words had been, I was trying to build a picture of the guy booting his daughter out of his house but not out of his life. He hadn't let go. He had spied on her. He'd followed her. She sees him at the restaurant and she thinks it's a come-home-baby-all-is-forgiven deal. Happy as larks, she jumps from me to him, but then it's not what she thought it would be. Ludwig Hofstetter is no longer Papa. He's become a couple of other things, like the avenging angel come to meet sin's payroll, not to speak of a sinner in his own right. She's put it up for grabs and he's risen in his righteousness to kill her for it, but while he's at it, he discovers that he's also one of the boys.

With a lot of straining I managed to think it could be possible but, no matter how hard I strained, I couldn't make it seem believable. I tried it another way. Perhaps he had been more than a father to her from way back, and all this chat about sin was no more than a cover-up for his jealous rage. She had left him for someone else, and for that he killed her. Thinking about it, I came to feel that, if anything, it made even less sense.

But that wasn't all. There was still the photographer's description. Straining again, I could imagine some complicated disguise that might have given Hofstetter the look that Gloria had described. It seemed to me that if there was anything you could call solid testimony in this whole business, it was Gloria's description of the man who wouldn't have his picture taken. The girl was in the business. She had a photographer's eye. She wouldn't be wrong in any detail.

I wondered whether any guy that heavily smitten with his body-beautiful vanity would, under any circumstances, go for a disguise. Would he conceal or falsify his great creation? I had a feeling that he wouldn't, not even for the most compelling reason.

Kicking it around, I couldn't work up any overwhelming faith in the psychological picture, and there was the question of height. I knew that elevator shoes could make a man look taller than he is, but I'd never had any experience with them. I didn't know what would be the maximum addition they could provide, but I could see no way that they could have added the three inches or more it would have taken to make little Ludwig look as though he stood anywhere in the vicinity of the six-foot range. It also occurred to me that Gloria had seen the man when he was sitting down. If she'd formed the impression of a tall man then, elevator shoes could hardly have been contributing to it. No guy sits at a restaurant table on his heels, and I'd never heard of elevator pants.

Cornered by this wide range of doubts, I tried thinking in terms of two men, the one who'd enjoyed her and the one who'd murdered her. I could think of no way of putting the evidence together that would have supported a two-man theory. The man seen in the restaurant had been the only loner in there at the time. He had been driving a car with Jersey plates and she had known him on sight. An accidental meeting? I couldn't believe it. The guy had been watching her and following her. So then, how can Daddy get in the act? Again I had to rule out accident.

I couldn't believe that he'd just happened to be in that vicinity that far from home and that he'd been precisely in time to see her with me, see her switch from me to this other guy, take her away from the other guy, and kill her. On the other hand, to think that both of them had followed us all the way from that stretch of road where I'd picked her up was impossible. I couldn't have driven all that distance as the leader of a parade and never have noticed anything. That even one car could have been on my tail throughout the whole of that journey without my once having been aware of it indicated some sneakily skillful tailing.

Okay. A guy is an old hand at this sort of operation. I can believe he's so good at it that he can fool Erridge. I can't believe that there could be that much expertise and all of it going only one way. I could have failed to notice I was being followed. The girl could also have failed to notice it, but of course it wasn't necessary to think that. She may well have noticed it and welcomed it. That she had noticed it by the time we were leaving the motel to go to dinner was obvious. That was when she'd begun acting up with me for his benefit.

I could leave her out of it. Whether she'd noticed at any time before that didn't matter. When she did become aware, she hadn't found it necessary to tell me. If she had known it earlier, it could be assumed that she wouldn't have found it any more necessary to tell me then.

I was thinking about the guy who had shown so much expertise in tailing me. I couldn't believe that such an expert could have gone without any awareness that he was not alone in sitting on Baby's tail.

There was also the question of what had become of this other man. Had he simply permitted Daddy to take her away from him and quietly gone off? Had our Ludwig killed the man as well and, leaving her body where it would incriminate me, disposed of the man's body elsewhere because he'd planned on her remains being found and on the man disappearing so completely that there'd be no indication that he'd ever been?

The more I tried to work it out, the more it came to seem the world's greatest exercise in futility. I could find no way to make sense of it. When I finally got to sleep that night, it was with a promise I made myself. I was going to find something to do, anything that could take my mind off Laura Hofstetter and what had happened to her.

Maybe I could have done it and maybe not. I was never given the chance to test it out. When I came down to breakfast, Mom switched off the kitchen radio and told me to get my orange juice out of the refrigerator. It was already squeezed and she'd had hers. For a while we were both too busy to talk. She was doing something wonderful for me with lamb kidneys and bacon while I was manning the toaster and the coffee pot.

When we did begin talking it was mostly me making appreciative noises over the kidneys. If Mom had had even the faintest notion of what she was doing, she'd never have said a word. She likes to see a man enjoy his food. She thinks that light and inconsequential conversation adds savor to a meal; but if talk at table is going to take away a man's appetite or even swing his attention too far from appreciation of what he's eating, she will have none of it. Under the delusion that she was being light and inconsequential, she spoke.

"Salvas, Matt," she said. "What kind of a name would you say that was? Salvas? I would guess it's spelled S-a-l-v-a-s. That's what it sounded like anyhow."

It meant nothing to me. I made a stab at answering her question.

"Probably Greek or Lithuanian," I said.

"Greek or Lithuanian? Are the languages that much alike? I shouldn't think they would be."

"I think they aren't," I said. "But you get hard-to-pronounce foreign names, like the Greek ones or the Lithuanian ones, and a man has to care a lot and have a lot of determination if he's going to keep it and not let it slip over into something an American tongue has less trouble getting around. Salvas, that sounds like one of those Americanizations. No matter how big the difference is in the original, the Americanizations get to sound pretty much the same."

"It's a disgrace," Mom said.

I shrugged it off.

"Their names get messed up?" I said. "They don't seem to mind. The ones that care about it fight it and win. The name gets mispronounced all over the place but they hang on to the spelling. Salvas? That the new kid you have helping in the garden?"

"No. He's easy. His name is Johnny, Johnny Rogers. This was on the radio just before you came down."

"A new pop singer or a new rock band?" I asked.

The question couldn't have been more idle. I certainly didn't care which or whether, but that's what light, inconsequential conversation is about. You don't care but you keep the ball in motion.

"No," Mom said. "It was on the news. Have you ever noticed those nasty, plastic-y bars along Route 9? They have glaring neon signs and everything else about them is drab and terribly, terribly dreary. I've always thought that drinking in one of them would be too depressing."

"Not if it's only a plastic look," I said. "It's when they sell plastic booze that you can get depressed."

"Have you ever been in any of them?" Mom asked.

"You know me. I get around."

I was beginning to have things like intimations and premonitions but I was careful not to let them show. It could be nothing and, even if it was something, I didn't want to worry Mom with it. For a moment I had the thought that the word gets around and someone had been telling Mom that her boy Matt had been having a fuss with a bartender in a Route 9 joint. That I could think it even for a moment was the result of my not having paid too close attention.

The thought didn't stay with me. Almost as quickly as I had it, I discarded it. In the first place, this kind of probing into what I might have been doing wasn't Mom's style, and then I did remember that she'd said something about its having come over the radio.

"It was a place called Nick's Tavern and that doesn't make much sense," Mom said. "They called him Gus Salvas and they said he owned the place. Wouldn't you think it would have been called Gus's Tavern?"

"Maybe there was a Nick once and the place changed hands. There isn't any Macy owning Macy's any more. What did the radio news have to say about it?"

"There was a fire last night. The place was completely destroyed, burned right down to the ground. They say there's nothing left of it and that it couldn't have been any ordinary sort of fire. They think it was a bomb. It blew the place up and set fire to the wreckage. They were talking about gangs. You know the way they go on and on when they don't know anything. Anyhow, they're looking for this Gus Salvas."

"He's missing?"

"They don't know. They think he might have been in the place when it went up. They're looking for a body, but they don't know. They also think he may be in hiding."

"Do they say he was mixed up in any gang stuff?" I asked.

"Gang war?" Mom said. "No, not like that. They said it might have been that he wouldn't pay for protection, or else it might have been that he'd been buying his liquor from one group and another group is moving in. If he refused to switch over to buying from these new people, they might have done this to make an example of him. They'll destroy one place to frighten all the others into coming in with them."

It seemed only fair that I should tell her before the word got around and some good friend hurried over to fill her in.

"I was in there yesterday," I said. "I had a little trouble with this guy Gus."

Mom's great. I doubt that there's another woman in the world who would have taken it the way she did. She said not a word about all the decent places I could go to do my drinking. There was enough of everything in the house. There was the golf club and the tennis club. There were pleasant and respectable bars all over the place, and if I had to go slumming I could have gone into the city for it, where it would be less likely that anyone would know me. Also, was it necessary for an Erridge to get himself involved in a vulgar brawl in a public place? If she thought any of that, she didn't even allow a trace of it to show in her voice and manner. She tossed nothing at me but sympathy, not the first hint of reproach.

"Oh, Matt!" she said. "What miserable luck! I hope this isn't going to be anything like it was with that unfortunate girl."

"She used to go there," I said. "He knew her."

She sighed.

"Poor Matt! I suppose it means that business must start up for you all over again."

"It never stopped," I said.

"Yes, I know, but at least you were out of it."

"Not really. I didn't ever feel out of it."

"You liked her, Matt?"

"I don't know. I didn't know her at all. I think I could have come to like her, but so much of the time we were together she was putting on an act that I don't have too much of an idea what she was really like."

"You went to this place because you felt you had to try to find out?"

"I went there because someone killed her and I can't get it out of my head that in some way he did it because of me."

"Jealousy, Matt?"

"No. All along it has seemed to me that there was more to it. Now I'm certain it was. Maybe they'll find Gus Salvas's body in the wreckage of his tavern and maybe he got away. I hope he got away, and if he did, I'm going to have to find a way to make him safe. I had trouble with him because he wouldn't tell me what he knew about the girl. I made him tell me something and Lord knows it wasn't much, but even for that his place was knocked over. If he's alive, it was a warning against saying anything ever again. If he's been killed, it was to guarantee that he would never talk again. It was also a warning to anyone else who might know anything."

"Then you'll have to tell this to the police."

"At least that. I can't leave it the way it is—that anyone who talks to Erridge dies."

"If she had a lover and she left him . . ." Mom began.

"She told me she had a husband and he left her," I said.

"He left her but he couldn't stand it that she didn't stay put to pine for him. There are more people like that than you think, Matt."

"And nobody who knew them is coming forward to tell who her husband or her lover or whatever he was might be. He's got to be more than just a jealous lover or a jealous husband to spread terror all over the place the way he obviously does."

"And even though this Salvas man didn't tell you, this swift and savage punishment?"

"He told me something. He told me where to find her father. I went around to see him. He raises roses and muscles."

"Mussels? As in *moules marinière?*"

"Muscles, as in triceps and biceps and bulges all over him."

"Like Mr. Universe?"

"Like that. A body-building nut."

"What did he say? Did he explain his not coming forward or anything?"

"He said the wages of sin are death."

"That's a misquotation," Mom said. "It should be 'the wages of sin *is* death.'"

"He also said she was no daughter of his."

"Did you believe that?"

"Couldn't be a stronger family resemblance. He meant he'd disowned her and he was damned if he was going to pay for her funeral."

"What a horrible man!"

"As screwy as a pig's tail."

"And with muscles? Violent?"

"He struck me as not. It seemed to me that the muscles were cultivated for ornament and not for use. They're like the roses. I complimented him on those and he jumped right in to tell me they weren't going to be flowers for her funeral."

"That's insane. A man *that* mad, he could have blown that tavern up last night just because the Salvas man told you this creature was the girl's father."

"I didn't tell him how I found out. I don't see how he could have known."

"If someone told him you'd been there," Mom suggested.

She might have had something.

"Or Salvas himself could have called him to warn him I would be around to talk to him," I said. "I can see this guy being an unforgiving nut. He's a great one for justice and for people getting what they have coming to them. He might have punished Salvas for telling me anything at all."

Mom sniffed. It wasn't a runny nose. It was disdain.

"A great one for justice," she said. "His daughter was murdered. What about bringing her murderer to justice?"

"Remember the wages of sin," I said. "Maybe he's thinking the murderer was the hand of God."

"Particularly if this fanatic murdered his own daughter."

"I've been thinking that, but I can't see any way it could work out."

I was about to fill her in, but I didn't get the time for it. We were interrupted. Through the windows I passed on my way to answer the doorbell I could see who it was. The police hadn't waited for me to come to them. They had come to me.

They were a great improvement on that earlier batch in West Virginia. They were armed. In our gun-happy country cops are always armed. The guns, however, remained holstered, and there weren't squad cars all over the place to keep the house covered from every angle. They didn't look in the least belligerent or even at the ready. They looked much as they do when they come around to sell tickets for the Policemen's Ball.

I opened the door to them. The new kid Mom had taken on to help her with her garden—she'd said his name was Johnny Rogers—was out there. He had been mowing the lawn but he'd stopped and was just sitting on the lawn mower gawping at the police. I noticed that he was about finished with the mowing, a square yard or two left to be cut, but no more than that. When I opened the door, he started the mower up again but only for one short spurt to finish that last bit of lawn.

There were two cops on the doorstep. One of them, a worried-looking type with two chins and fat creases in his neck, spoke for the two of them. He introduced himself as Sergeant Meek and told me the other one was Officer Landrum.

"I heard at breakfast," I said. "I was about to come to see you, but the news gets around fast."

"We had it from Pennsylvania," the sergeant said.

I hadn't expected that.

"They knew out there?"

"They said you called and told them."

It took me a few moments to get that sorted out in my head. I asked the officers to come in and I used the time while Mom was offering them coffee to untangle my thinking. It was simple enough. I'd called Pennsylvania with a full account of my time at Nick's Tavern and my visit to Ludwig Hofstetter. I had held out nothing from them except any mention of young Bert.

So Pennsylvania has been through to the local cops with a request that they check out things at this end. The Pennsylvania request hits smack up against the arson at Nick's Tavern. The thing had fitted together automatically.

The sergeant asked the questions and Officer Landrum took down everything that was said. I had nothing to tell them that they didn't already know, since I'd given Pennsylvania a full run-down and they'd had a complete fill-in from them. For what it was worth, they were getting the whole thing all over again, but they wanted it straight out of my mouth. When Landrum had his shorthand transcribed, he was going to bring the transcription around for me to sign. They had evidently come with no idea of having anything more from me than they already knew. They had come around only because they had to have it in the form of a signed statement. There was much apology for putting me to the trouble of going through all of it again. The sergeant was more than polite. He was deferential.

He told me more than I could tell him. Both the tavern and Hofstetter's house were in other towns, but all the local police forces worked together. The sergeant had been talking to his opposite numbers in those other towns. He had background on Salvas and on Hofstetter.

There wasn't much on Salvas. He had a wife but they'd been separated for more than a year.

"He has no kind of a record at all," the sergeant said. "You told that DA over in Pennsy that he'd been selling to minors. The police over his way knew nothing about that."

"That," Mom interjected, "could be only because they didn't want to know."

"Yes, ma'am," the sergeant said, "but the way it is over that way, the fellows they've got their hands full with marijuana and heroin. They can't be everywhere all the time. They've got to let the small stuff get by."

"I know." Mom was implacable. "And they're so busy handing out traffic tickets. I'm sure that wears them out."

"Yes, ma'am," the sergeant said.

Before he would have to cope with any more of that, he did a quick switch to what he'd picked up from his colleagues in Hofstetter's area.

"That one," he said. "He's a nut."

"Any record?" I asked.

"No police record, but the guys over there know him. It's not like anybody has anything against religion, but he's a case. All the churches over that way—the priests, the ministers, the rabbis, he's always writing them these dirty letters. It's like he's more religious than anybody. None of the churches are holy enough for him. He writes them these letters calling them names. 'Money-changers in the temple.' That's the only one I can say before a lady."

"Don't mind me," Mom told him. "If there were any words I didn't learn from my husband, I've learned them from my son. There can't be any I haven't heard."

Apart from blushing till his ears turned crimson, the sergeant pretended that she hadn't said anything.

"Just letters?" I asked. "No violence?"

"Only letters."

"What's with the body-building? He could be in training for the Mr. America contest."

The sergeant shrugged.

"He don't smoke. He don't drink. His wife's been dead now twenty years, and he didn't marry again and he never goes near a woman. I suppose a man has to do something with himself."

"Like falling in love with his own body," I said.

The sergeant's blushes had just about faded out. Now he stole a glance at Mom and, as the crimson came flooding back, he tossed me a reproachful look. In his way of thinking, I was talking dirty before a lady.

I could see that Mom was about to make her own contribution to the conversation and I expected it was going to be rough on the sergeant's sense of decorum. The sergeant must have had similar expectations. Along with its color his face took on an apprehensive look. Officer Landrum, younger and with longer hair, was grinning over his steno pad.

Mom, however, never did get to say what she might have had in mind. Johnny Rogers came in from his yard work and knocked off any further discussion of the redoubtable Ludwig's peculiarities.

"Excuse me, sir," he said. "Could you come outside with me for a minute?"

Mom came up out of her chair.

"Mr. Erridge is busy," she said. "I'll go, Johnny."

Johnny retreated to the door but only to plant himself in it and bar Mom's way.

"Please, Mrs. Erridge. You better stay in the house."

There was something wrong about the kid. For any question about lawn or garden there was too much urgency in his voice. There was also the way he looked. He was pouring sweat. You could expect that. After all, he had been working out in the sun for what had been the better part of what was becoming the first hot morning we'd had that year, but it wasn't that kind of sweat. It looked like a cold sweat. The kid was white-faced, even white-lipped.

I could think of only two possibilities. It could have been that he'd been taken suddenly sick and with embarrassing symptoms he was desperately trying to keep from Mom, or else it would have to be that he had let the lawn mower go out of control and had destroyed one of Mom's prize flowerbeds and now he didn't dare let her see it without first getting me to break the news to her.

I had to take the poor kid off the hook. It occurred to me that at the same time I could relieve Sergeant Meek of his embarrassment.

"If you gentlemen want to come with me," I suggested, "we can go on with this outside."

As though Johnny wasn't looking troubled enough already, my suggestion obviously made things worse. He turned on me the most eloquent look of dismay. There was no help for it. Officer Landrum was gathering up his pad and pencils, and with the greatest alacrity Sergeant Meek was heading for the doorway young Johnny was occupying with his Horatius-at-the-bridge act. For a moment it looked as though we were headed for one of those immovable-object-irresistible-force collisions, but at the last moment the immovable object surrendered to necessity. Johnny stepped aside.

As soon as we were outside with the door shut behind us, Sergeant Meek stopped.

"I didn't want to talk about it where the lady could hear," he said. "Salvas's wife is living in Newark with a guy named Floyd Parsons. Salvas has been shacking up in Elizabeth with the Parsons guy's wife."

I laughed.

"Where have you been, Sergeant?" I said. "That's just the kind of thing the ladies talk about over the bridge table."

The sergeant frowned.

"Not *my* wife," he said. "Not my wife and not my mother. *They* don't."

I could have asked him if he'd like to bet, but it seemed to be too important to him. I decided that I'd leave him with his delusions. I turned to Johnny.

"What's the problem?" I asked.

"Could I talk to you alone a minute, sir? There's something I've got to show you."

I turned to Sergeant Meek.

"Sure," he said. "Go ahead. Take your time."

So far as I could see, the garden had suffered no disaster. The lawn was all mowed and the mower had been put away. At one corner of the swimming pool the winter cover had been unfastened and rolled back. I grinned. That's the way Mom operates. Since we were heading into a hot day, she'd immediately thought that her boy, Matthew, might want a swim. She'd told Johnny to take the cover off the pool, clean it and fill it. There isn't much a man could ever want for his comfort that he won't find Mom has anticipated it.

Johnny led the way toward the pool.

"Okay," I said. "It can't be as bad as you think it is. It never is. What's your problem?"

"The pool," Johnny whispered. "That corner where the cover's off. Mrs. Erridge said to get the pool ready this morning. When I went to take the cover off it wasn't fastened down the way it ought to be. At that one corner it wasn't. Somebody'd had it off at that corner and didn't put it back on tight the way it ought to be. When I turned the loose corner back and looked in, I saw him. He's down in there."

I tried to think it would be some crazy drunk who'd come by in the night and, turning back the cover at that corner, had taken a skull-smashing dive into the empty pool. The thought, of course, wouldn't stand up. Johnny hadn't said he'd found the corner of the pool uncovered. He'd only said he'd found the cover not properly fastened at that corner. Also, that much I'd seen for myself. Before going down to breakfast I'd gone to the window and looked out at the day.

From my window I'd looked straight down on the pool. From upstairs I couldn't see whether the cover was properly fastened all around but I had seen the pool completely covered. No part of the cover had been turned back then. If there was someone down in there, then it had to follow that he hadn't fallen in or dived in or, at least if he had, there had been someone with him, someone who pulled the cover back over the pool and went away.

We were only a few yards away from it and, if I didn't cover the distance in one jump, I can't remember ever touching ground en route. I looked in and he was there. You could read the body like a book.

It was, or it had been, Gus Salvas. He wasn't far down. He had been dumped in at the shallow end and he was dead. Nobody lives when his skull has been that much caved in. Just looking down at the body, I knew right off that the kind of skull damage I was seeing hadn't come just from his being dumped into the empty pool and landing on his head. His skull had taken multiple blows. It had been worked over with a baseball bat or a length of lead pipe. Glancing back at Sergeant Meek and Officer Landrum where they were waiting for me near the house, I added an item to my list of possible weapons. Or a police billy club, I thought.

I thought it only in passing. There were other things about the body that caught my attention. Except for a pair of jockey shorts it was naked, and even the shorts were somewhat less than complete. What there was of them was scorched and smoke-stained, and in great patches the body's skin showed a peculiar discoloration. Never having seen anything like it before, I had to make a guess at what it was, but it was an easy guess. Burns on a dead man's body might well look like that. If there could have been any doubt of it, the smell would have settled it. The smell was there and it was unmistakably the smell of burned flesh and scorched hair.

It came through to me only gradually that Johnny was talking to me. I turned to him and listened.

"Want I should put the cover back on till they're gone?" he was asking.

IX.

It was, of course, the same deal all over again, so much the same deal that it had to be the same killer. The only thing about it that was different was the way the police treated me this time around. Here in my home territory where I was known and where Erridges had been known since way back when, there was no rough stuff. There wasn't even the first move toward taking me in.

I did have more going for me than just my local reputation and my family record of respectability. I called Meek and Landrum right over and showed them the body. Nobody could say I tried to cover anything up and nobody could think, as they had in the girl's case, that I'd tried to run. I'd already furnished the police with a full account of my encounters with Salvas and Hofstetter.

Furthermore, there was no need to wait for any autopsy results before we could know what the body had to tell us. He had run out of the burning tavern in his scorched shorts and seared skin. Someone had been waiting for him outside, taking no chance on his escaping the fire. It could have been nowhere but there, right outside the burning tavern, that he had run into the baseball-bat or lead-pipe job. Obviously he had been killed in those first moments before any of the fire trucks arrived.

Obviously also, it had been a time when disposing of the body couldn't have been easier. For a killer who might have hoped to erase any evidence of how Salvas had died, there would have been nothing needed but to pick up the body and heave it into the flames of the burning building. For a killer who was not concerned about leaving evidence of the manner of death, there would have been nothing at all to do. He could have left the body where it lay, right there in the spot where Salvas had fallen under the killer's blows.

The killer hadn't been satisfied with that. He'd walked away from his easy outs and had gone to a lot of trouble and to tremendous risk in carting the body all the way to the swimming pool. Not content even with that, he'd hung on in the garden, multiplying the hazards, while he unfastened the corner of the pool cover and heaved the body in.

The first time around, his motives for trying to throw the guilt on me had been obvious. Then as now, he had gone to a great deal of trouble and risk in carrying it out, but then he'd had a situation where he'd had every expectation that he could frame Erridge and that Erridge would stay framed, putting him in the clear.

Furthermore, the risk involved in bringing her body back to the motel to dump it in the bushes there, and in getting into the room to leave her clothes under the bed, had been only a plus added on to the trouble and risk he had evidently been forced to take in any case.

Those two dirty and worn ten-dollar bills had come to loom large in my thinking. At first it had seemed to me that the foremost reason for going back to the motel and sneaking into the room while I slept had not been those two tens. I had been thinking that the killer, once he was there, had picked the tens up in passing. Now I'd come around to the idea that the killer had had to get them back into his hands. He couldn't risk leaving them with me. Those two bills had been special. They'd had some importance distinct from their simple monetary value.

So now the question was, Why this second time? On this one, by no stretch of the imagination could the killer have thought that by bringing the body home to me and dumping it into my pool he could set me up as the prime suspect for the killing.

The picture he had built with Laura's body and Laura's clothes back there at the motel had been one of a drunken and disorganized Erridge going through some such performance as stripping the girl in the motel room, raping and killing her, and then carrying the body out to hide it in the bushes. Because he was drunk, however, he failed to remember that he had neglected to remove the girl's incriminating clothes from the room when he had removed the body.

My going after him and locking myself out of the room naked, of course, had not been anything he had engineered. That had been a bit of luck that played into his hands to make the picture more convincing.

His carefully constructed frame had not held up, but it had failed only because of the timing of my movements and the gas station man's corroboration of that timing, and because of some of the physiological aspects of death that, since he'd been ignorant of them, he had been unable to cover in his scheme.

With this second body the situation had been reversed. If I had been the killer at the motel, I would have had excellent reason for getting the body out of my room. If I had been the killer at the tavern, however, I would have had the body at a place where its location would be least likely to throw suspicion in my direction. Even if I had been drunk and fumbling around, it would still have been impossible for me to have formed the delusion that there could be any advantage for me in carting Salvas's body home and leaving it to be found in my swimming pool.

The first had been a frame that came close to working. This was a situation that screamed "frame" so emphatically that the body, being where it was, couldn't possibly incriminate me. If anything, it cleared me.

I couldn't believe he wouldn't have known that such was going to be the result. So that raised the big question. Why? I didn't have to do much pondering on it. The answer seemed obvious. The murderer was throwing me signals.

I had questioned Gus Salvas and I'd got next to nothing out of him. That night Salvas's place is blown up and burned down and Salvas is clubbed to death. Such reprisals seemed excessive for the little Salvas had told me. Having got so little from him, I might have missed the point of the bombing and the arson and the killing. I might have assumed that Salvas's murder had nothing to do with me, that he hadn't been killed because he'd talked to me or even to prevent his telling me more in the event that I might bring further pressure. I might have thought that Salvas had been in some totally unrelated trouble.

It had been important to the killer that I develop no such delusions. The body in the swimming pool was telling me that it was because he'd talked to me that Salvas had been killed. I was being warned to lay off, to ask no more questions. If I hadn't recognized that I was up against tough opposition, the body had been put there to tell me.

It was hours before I could break away from the police. I wasn't put under arrest and at no point did anyone treat me as a suspect, but I was answering questions and making signed statements. Mom and Johnny, of course, were similarly tied up, but for them it was only a relatively brief questioning. Had Mom heard or seen anything during the night? She hadn't. Had I? I hadn't. When had Johnny come to work? Eight o'clock in the morning. Had he noticed anything? He hadn't. Why had he looked into the pool?

It was that sort of thing for the three of us, but the questions put to Mom and Johnny stopped in that area. Mine moved out to the other places. What had happened the day before in the tavern? What had passed between me and Hofstetter?

Once they had the body, of course, it was no longer just Sergeant Meek and Officer Landrum. It was battalions of cops. I'd never imagined that our peaceful little community could be so cop-heavy. As the morning wore on, I began to get the message. They weren't all ours. Squads of them had come over from the Nick's Tavern area.

Talking with them I became more and more convinced that, without exception, they were taking the wrong slant on this whole affair. I began by thinking they were too stupid to see the obvious and I tried to show them, to push them into some recognition of the way the two murders hung together. When it came to me that it wasn't only that they couldn't see it but that they couldn't be made to see it, I found myself doubting their stupidity. They were *too* blind. It didn't seem possible. It wasn't that they couldn't see. They were determined not to.

They had a murder on their hands and they were working on that. They weren't going to let themselves get involved with two murders. The theory on which they persisted in working had it that out there in western Pennsylvania the girl had picked up some stranger, just as earlier she had picked up Erridge, another stranger. They argued that her killer had been some local out there.

A traveler, they said, would have had no need to go through all that risky stuff he'd done in an effort to pin the killing on me. He could have just moved on. Only a local would have needed a scapegoat, and who better for that role than this guy in the Porsche with whom she had been making herself conspicuous?

They weren't quite saying that I brought these things on myself, but the implication was there. They wouldn't see the Salvas murder as anything but a gang killing. The body in my pool? They set that down to a clumsy effort to make the killing look like something it wasn't. Erridge had done it again. He had gone to Nick's Tavern and had hassled Gus Salvas, and Salvas's gang enemies had jumped at the opportunity. They would do as that killer out in Pennsylvania had done. This guy Erridge, he goes over to Nick's and makes a big public show just the same way as he made a big public show in that restaurant, loving up the girl all through their meal. Let's put the cops to looking at him. They'll be so busy with the golf-club set and the tennis-club set that they'll never look at us, the backroom set.

In all their thinking they were leaving out the one inexplicable item—those two old and dirty ten-dollar bills. I spoke of them to Sergeant Meek and he dismissed them all too glibly. It was obvious that the point had come up earlier and an official line had been established on it. He was politely careful about the way he fed it to me, but what it came to was that this guy Erridge had been drinking too much and having the girl run out on him the way she did had kicked him in the gut. So, what with the one thing and another, he'd gone through that night not making much sense.

There hadn't been any burglar. There had just been a visitor come to deliver the dead girl's clothes. Erridge, not aware that there had been a delivery, could think nothing but a burglary. When he checked to see what had been taken, he had been confused, not yet having slept off all the drink he had soaked up. What could be more natural than that he should fasten on those two tens, forgetting that in a drunken rage he had thrown them away or even that he had quite simply spent them.

"Anyone who took the twenty bucks would have taken all you had in your wallet," Sergeant Meek said.

"That's just the point," I argued. "Those two tens weren't taken for their money value. There was something else about them."

The sergeant laughed.

"Maybe over this way where all you rich folks live," he said, "you can forget the money value of money. The rest of us can't."

It would have been no good protesting that I hadn't been that drunk. I'd run out of the motel room bare-ass naked, hadn't I? Could I call that sobriety?

On the pretext of needing to use the men's room, I pulled away from the cops for a few minutes. Ordinarily I would have gone to the downstairs john, but that time I was responding to more than the demands of my bladder. I'd had an idea. I went up to my room and used my own bathroom. I pulled two tens out of my billfold. They weren't nearly old enough or dirty enough, but I knew how to handle that. It was why I had gone upstairs. My tens needed antiquing.

I worked on the oldest pair I had, crumpling them up, dropping them to the floor, walking back and forth on them. It wasn't enough. They needed more than that. I'd expected they would. This much I could have done in the downstairs john. I rummaged in the bathroom cupboard and found what I wanted, a can of black shoe polish. With the blacking I did a quick but careful job. It took only a couple of smears of the stuff, another crumpling and a little more walking up and down on them. That did it. Smoothed out they looked good enough. I didn't return them to my billfold. I crumpled them again and put them in my pants pocket. After I'd washed the shoe polish off my hands, I went back downstairs. I had a new line to try on the cops.

I began with Sergeant Meek. I knew they had their job to do and I didn't want anybody to scant anything. I was just hoping that they'd recognize how hard this whole thing was on Mom.

"You know how the ladies are. They get upset."

I was, of course, careful to say it only when Mom wasn't around to hear me. She's never been a dedicated women's libber, but it would take no more than that to push her into it.

All the time I was feeding him this stuff, I had my pair of antiqued tens in my hand. I was toying with them. I wasn't offering him a bribe. I was just holding the bills where they were available. All he needed to do was take them out of my hand. He didn't touch them and he gave them no attention, even though it wasn't possible that he should not be seeing them.

By this time I knew that the contingent that had come over from the other town was led by Chief Harrison. The chief was nothing like genial and easygoing Sergeant Meek. This was a lean guy, rawhide tough, somewhere in his mid-forties. He looked competent, both sharp and mean. For our peaceful district the affable Meek did well enough. There really wasn't much for him to do beyond sitting around and waiting to inherit the earth.

That stretch where Route 9 runs through the chief's district is another story. It is a high crime area. They might well have needed a hard-nosed cop over there.

Meek promised he would do all he could. He was even more solicitous of Mom than I ever could be or could even pretend to be.

Chief Harrison was something else again. He took notice of the bills in my hand. He took so much notice of them that I doubted that he was even hearing what I was saying to him. He didn't reach for the tens. He didn't so much as touch them but, try as he would to disguise his interest, he couldn't keep his eyes off them.

All the time I was making this pitch, Mom's impulses toward hospitality were taking over. She kept coffee going in the kitchen. At the first opportunity she'd brought out the big coffee maker and set it going. Repeatedly she passed the word through our swarm of cops: there was coffee in the kitchen. They were just to go in and help themselves whenever they might feel like it. At one moment she buttonholed me.

"Don't you think you should set up a bar, Matthew?"

"For them? They don't drink on duty."

"Don't they?"

"They shouldn't."

I was expecting that she would ask the lot of them to stay to lunch, but they didn't stick around that long. It was a little after eleven when they pulled out.

I told Mom to pack a bag. I was taking her into New York.

"Whatever for?" she asked.

"A New York binge," I said. "Running barefoot through Bonwit's. All the things you've been planning to do there and haven't gotten around to."

"Another time, Matthew. Right now in the spring I can't leave the garden."

"Johnny will look after the garden. Leave it for another time and you'll have to do it alone. Now you can do it with me."

That made all the difference. She knew why I wanted her away from the house, and as long as she'd thought I'd be shipping her off and staying to hold the fort alone, she had been ready to dig in and make every excuse for staying with me. Once I'd made it clear that we'd both be going, she was able to think of it as taking her boy Matthew away from whatever might be threatening. Immediately it had become a great idea.

She tested it out.

"You hate shopping," she said.

"I hate shopping," I agreed. "I have my own things to do, and while I'm doing them you can shop, catch some shows, have a ball."

I didn't say anything about where those things I had to do were going to take me and she didn't ask. If she had any suspicions, and I'm sure she did, she didn't say. She's a tactful woman.

There was one other thing I had to set up and I didn't know how she was going to take it.

"I don't think we should leave the house empty," I said.

"It won't be the first time it's been empty. It'll be all right."

I wished I could have left it like that, but the signal had been thrown and I couldn't guess what would come next. I was carrying around mental pictures of what had been done to Nick's Tavern and I knew that Mom could never say it's only a house and there would always be other houses. It was her house. My old man had been born in that house. He'd brought her to it as a bride. No other house would ever be the same for her. I couldn't take any chances with it.

"It's the first time anybody used the swimming pool for anything but swimming," I said.

"You think?"

What I was thinking I didn't want to put into words for her.

"I think we should have somebody house-sitting while we're gone," I said.

"We could speak to Johnny," she said. "He's a good, reliable boy."

I told her I'd do it while she packed. When I spoke to him, I told him a lot more than I'd told her.

"It'll be all right in the daytime," I said. "Nobody will try anything by daylight as long as you're around. The way this guy is playing it, he's being very careful not to be seen. If he comes around it'll be at night, and I'll have someone here with you for the nights."

"I'll be okay," Johnny said.

"You'll need to sleep sometime," I told him. "The night watch will call for a pro. He'll do the watching. You'll be here just so Mom won't feel she's turned her house over to a stranger."

"Don't let Mrs. Erridge worry," Johnny said. "I'll take care of the place."

"She knows you will," I said. "She told me to talk to you."

I phoned around and got on to a good agency that provides security guards for temporary tours of duty. They took on the job, promising a man at the house before dark. The guards were to be kept on in shifts till I called them off.

I drove Mom into town but I used her car. There was too good a chance that Baby might have been set up as a target. I was ready to take my chances in her alone and I thought it likely that I would have to, but I wasn't going to take any of those risks with Mom. She knows that her wheels bore me and she brought it up.

"You don't enjoy driving my car and you get itchy riding while someone else drives, and I don't at all mind riding in the Porsche," she said.

"Not this time," I told her. "This is your party. We do it your style."

In the city I checked us in at the club. She likes it, and with her there I'd have nothing to worry about. All kinds of people can turn up in hotels. I had told her I was going to be tied up all afternoon and evening, and she had phoned friends and was all fixed up for dinner and the evening. Until then she was hitting the shops. I took off on the business I had to do.

It was a cab to the bus terminal and a bus back out home. There I dug out a gun I had and stuck it into the waistband of my slacks. Picking up Baby, I started on my rounds. On what the sergeant had told me about the Salvas-Parsons wife swap I saw little chance that I would be able to find the lady in Elizabeth. If it turned out that I needed to find her, it was likely that my best bet would be at Gus Salvas's funeral.

Meanwhile I was heading for Newark and Salvas's wife. You have to know about Newark. There was a time not too many years ago when it was a good enough sort of city. Even though it's the largest city in the state, it's too close to New York ever to have seemed anything but a small place. For some time now it has been a sick city, one of the sickest in the country, and the people who are living there now, if they are not helpless souls who have no place else to go, are brave and optimistic, hanging on in the hope of a turn for the better, or they are an integral part of the decay, more at home in the city's corruption than they ever could be in some decent place.

I pulled into a gas station and checked the phone book. There was only one Floyd Parsons listed. I rolled around to the address. The street had once been a good one. The houses were not so old that they would be anybody's landmark, but they were old enough to have been solidly built and generously laid out. There were lawns and an occasional tree. Attached to some of the houses there was even a bit of a garden, and some showed the overgrown and tangled remains of what had once been a garden.

A few of the houses and their surrounding plots had been decently kept up, but most of them sat in patches of weeds littered with refuse. Their porches sagged. Their paint was peeling. Their unwashed windows were broken and had been patched with masking tape. The houses were what used to be considered family-size, but the decaying ones looked as though they now housed several families.

The Parsons house stood somewhere between the valiantly preserved and the decaying. Its porch didn't sag and the windows were clean. The house needed painting but only because the paint had gone dingy. Alongside its decrepit neighbors it looked great. The lawn also had the in-between look. It needed cutting and a good part of it had been taken over by crabgrass and dandelions, but unlike its neighbors, it wasn't knee-high and it hadn't been used as a dump.

All up and down the street where cars stood in the short driveways there were jalopies in a state of decay that matched the houses. The few places that looked well kept up had no cars standing in their driveways. That was easy to figure. If they didn't belong to guys who had driven them to work, they would be locked away in the garages where they were safe from car thieves and vandals. I could picture the kind of cars they would be—lovingly maintained minijobs or well-preserved oldies.

Nobody could picture the car that stood in the Parsons driveway. It was a late-model pink Cadillac and it didn't have so much as a scratch on it. Just sitting out there where anyone could get at it, that pink Caddy spoke to me. Whether it belonged to Parsons or it was a visitor's car, it was the property of somebody formidable. Its owner commanded fear and respect, and his power was so well known in the neighborhood that nobody would be taking any risks with it.

I turned into the driveway and I parked Baby behind the pink mammoth. I was gambling that I was not leaving her in too great jeopardy. I had a hunch that I was leaving her on forbidden ground. Going past the Caddy on my way to the house, I noticed that her doors were monogrammed. FP. Owning a car like that, Floyd Parsons wasn't living on that street because he needed a lot of house at low cost. I was guessing that he lived there because it was his base of operations.

I mounted the porch steps and rang the doorbell. It was a politely brief ring, none of that leaning on the bell and staying with it stuff. Even at that, however, the door was opened before I had my finger off the bell. Maybe the lady just happened to be at the door when I rang, or maybe she had been watching my approach.

The lady was a redhead in a sweater and stretch pants, and she was stretching both the sweater and the pants to the limits of their elasticity. Apart from the bulging prominence of her various and sundry erogenous zones, her most arresting feature was her eyes. They were so heavily befurred with fake eyelashes that she could have had nothing but an English sheepdog's view of the world. The eyelashes were backed up with great smears of eyeshadow. I've never seen a woman with gangrened eyelids but, seeing her, I knew what they would look like.

"Hello, Matt," she said.

If she hadn't learned to talk at Mae West's knee, there would have been no way she could have made it sound the way she did.

"Hello," I said.

I left it at that because I didn't know whether etiquette would require that I call her Mrs. Salvas or Mrs. Parsons.

"Louella," she said and she batted the eyelashes at me.

I had a moment of wondering whether, being a Louella, she had been automatically attracted to a Parsons or if she had only assumed the name to go with her present station. The eyelash-batting was something to watch. She had muscle in her eyelids. If I hadn't seen her do it, I would never have thought that, once she'd dropped them, she could ever again hoist up their eyelash weight.

"Hello, Louella."

"Don't just stand there, Matt. Come in and take a load off your feet."

I followed her into the living room. Seen from behind, her walk was an anatomical impossibility. It could be done only with ball bearings. She dropped into a corner of a sofa that was as overstuffed as were her sweater and pants and she patted the seat beside her. I settled in.

"You know who I am," I said.

"You're the one who found Gus's body. You're Matthew Erridge. It's nice of you to come around, but I'm not in mourning."

"And you're not afraid to talk to me?"

"You didn't kill him. You'd have to be a dope to take the body home with you. That's crazy."

"He talked to me," I said. "That may be why he's dead."

"Yeah. He put you on to her crazy old man. He had ought to've known better than that."

"You knew Laura and you know her father?"

"She used to hang around Gus."

"And all the time she went unidentified nobody said anything. That's what I can't understand."

"Gus talked to you. So Gus is dead and I'm alive."

"Everyone who knew her was afraid to say a word. Why? Who's got you so scared?"

She laughed.

"Tell me, Matt. Are you that dumb or do you just play dumb?"

"I'm that dumb. You'll have to tell me."

She told me. Everyone who had known Laura knew her father and everyone knew his story. Once, way back before the girl was born, he'd been an ordinary sort of guy. Then the girl's birth had changed everything.

"Something went wrong," she said. "It don't happen much any more, but it used to happen quite a lot. They saved the baby but his wife died. That's when he went nuts. Maybe he was religious before. I don't know. But then he went crazy religious. Sex is a sin and she died because she'd sinned with him."

"What about *him*? Didn't he sin with her. It's no one-way street."

"It sure ain't. Doesn't everybody with somebody? I told you he went crazy. He's been crazy ever since. When the kid grew up and she started to live like everybody else, he threw her out. She wasn't his daughter. She never was his daughter. All that crap."

"I never saw a father and daughter who looked more alike."

She shrugged.

"Sure, but maybe he was kidding himself that it wasn't *his* sin, that his wife was with someone else. Who knows what a crazy man might think?"

And that was it. Ludwig Hofstetter had killed his daughter and he had everyone who had ever known the girl terrorized.

"He thought he could put it on you. And then, when he killed Gus, he thought he could put that on you. He's crazier than a bedbug."

"What about her husband?" I asked.

"What husband?"

"She told me that she had a husband and he had just walked out on her."

"Look. She was crazy, too. Not like her old man, but what could you expect? All the time she was growing up, all the time in that house with only him, she had to grow up a little crazy.

She was always telling stories. Maybe she even believed them herself. You grow up the way she did, never having anything the other girls had. Maybe she grew up just having what she made up in her head, like a husband she didn't have anyplace else, only in her head."

It was a good story and it wasn't. It left out too much. It left out the man with the Hollywood face and the Hollywood build and the mole on his left cheek. It left out those two ten-dollar bills.

I brought my two tens out of my pocket. I didn't shove them at her. I just held them in my hands, folding them and unfolding them. She saw them and she was careful to look away. She turned her head toward the door and she shouted.

"Floyd, honey," she called. "We got company. Come and meet Matt Erridge. Come and fix Matt a drink."

X.

Maybe it was a crazy time to be thinking about Mom and to be harking way back to the time when she was working on my manners, but Floyd honey was about to come into the room to meet me, and it's bad manners to sit tight and let the other guy stand over you. You get to your feet. You also don't remain seated when a lady rises. That much I'd learned from Mom.

There was also what I had learned on my own. Anytime you are faced with the possibility of enemy action, it's smart to be up off your ass. You're giving yourself a wider range of options. Floyd honey was an unknown quantity. It was just possible that he might be the beautiful man with the mole on his left cheek. We had been followed, Laura and me, and she hadn't known it until we were leaving the motel to go to dinner. For a guy who drives a pink Cadillac a nondescript hired heap would have been a great disguise as long as he stayed behind the wheel.

It was time to play the gentleman and I tried. Honest, Mom, I did try.

I had too much to contend with. There was Louella and there was the overstuffed sofa. You know those squishy upholstery jobs. They're a menace. They are too close to the floor to give a man the best leverage, and they offer nothing solid you can push against. Louella made it because she'd laid a loving hand on my thigh, and that gave her what I didn't have—something solid to push against.

"Don't get up," she said. "Floyd never knows where anything is."

He came in at that moment. She wasn't altogether right about him. He knew where Erridge was. He was a big guy, bigger than my photographer friend back at the restaurant had described. He had a flat nose and some little lines of scar around his eyes. Just in case that lady's taste might be peculiar, I looked for the mole. He didn't have one.

He was wearing nothing but a pair of briefs. That was great for seeing he was a powerful guy who kept himself in top shape. It was even better for seeing that he was clean of any lethal weapon. There was no place on him where he could be concealing a knife or a gun or anything he could use as a club.

"Glad to see you, Matt," he said.

I pushed against the squishy cushions, making another try at getting to my feet, but now he was in position for dealing with it. A beefy hand on my shoulder pushed me back down.

"Don't get up," he said. "Lou'll bring in the fixings and we'll hoist a few."

He stood over me and he stood with his hands at the ready. He wasn't making fists, nothing like that, but he was poised for those little shoves that would work in conjunction with the sofa to make Erridge sit and to keep him sitting. I did what I could. I slid over to that corner of the sofa Louella had just vacated. It wasn't much good, but it had one advantage. It put me in position for seeing out the window. It put me where I could keep an eye on Baby.

I know that sounds crazy. Here I was in a spot where I should have been thinking about myself, and I'm telling you that the first thing I had on my mind was the Porsche.

Louella and Floyd were dead set on keeping me where I was. I couldn't believe it was no more than warmhearted hospitality. Whatever it was, it was triggered by my two tens. I still had them in my hand and Floyd wasn't as shy as Louella. He was making no pretense of not seeing them.

So they were holding me where I was. They had me waiting for something. There were all sorts of possibilities. Not the least of them was the time it might take for someone out in their driveway to wire a bomb to Baby's ignition. I was watching for that. There was nobody out there.

Another possibility was that Louella had stepped out to fix

me a mickey. You can have a well-stocked bar and not have any chloral hydrate in your bar stocks, but I was not about to take any bets on Floyd Parsons' bar being without it.

The big man reached down and took the two tens out of my hand. He held them until Louella came back in. She was wheeling a fancy bar cart. It was heavily loaded: an ice bucket, a jug of water, unopened bottles of club soda, tonic, ginger ale, coke, and beer; scotch, Bourbon, rye, vodka, rum, gin, and cognac; lemons, limes, tabasco, Worcestershire, bitters, and grenadine.

She wheeled the cart so close to me that she only barely missed rolling it onto my foot. That was the foot big Floyd was only barely missing standing on. I had been well hemmed in by Floyd alone. Now I was totally barricaded.

"You know how you like it, Matt," she said. "Maybe you'd like to fix your own."

It could have been the custom of the house, but I had a hunch that it wasn't. They knew I'd be thinking mickey. It was a way of putting the thought out of my head. I picked up a glass, bypassing the one that stood nearest me and reaching across for another one. I took a moment away from keeping an eye on Baby to have a good look at the glass and make certain I was starting off with an empty one. It was empty.

I was about to reach for the Bourbon and the water, but before I moved my hand I was thinking better of it. The word could have been passed, that was what I'd been drinking the day before in Nick's Tavern. The Bourbon wasn't my brand, but it was good bonded stuff and that could be one way of doing it. Fix the Bourbon and fix the water. If the guy's suspicious, you take care of that by letting him mix his own. With that array of stuff available, it's no problem for host and hostess to drink with their guest. All they need to do is stick with another tipple.

I poured myself the drink and I made it scotch and soda. I'm not so confirmed a Bourbon drinker that I can't take scotch. Ordinarily I don't want my drinks fizzy because it gets in the way of tasting the whiskey, but whatever I had come there for, it wasn't to taste whiskey.

Louella fixed one for Floyd and it was a duplicate of mine, out of the same whiskey bottle and out of the same soda bottle. For herself it was rye and ginger ale. I suppose that made her an old-fashioned girl. She left the bar cart where it was, tight against my knee, and now with their drinks they were both standing over me.

Floyd proposed the toast.

"To his rotting in jail," he said.

"It won't be the slammer for him," Louella said. "He's for the loony bin, him with his muscles and his roses and his crazy ideas."

She made the correction, but she drank to it anyway. I made my own correction.

"To justice," I said.

They didn't seem to mind. They were ready to let me have that my own way. Floyd waved my two tens.

"Have a look at these," he said to Louella. "Look at the dirty money this guy carries on him."

She took the two bills and set down her drink. She needed both her hands for smoothing the two tens out so that she could examine them closely. Shaking her head, she handed them back to me. The head-shaking could have been disapproval, but it was too obvious that Floyd had been watching for it. It was a signal. She was letting him know that the bills weren't what they'd been thinking they might be.

"Somebody gives me money like that," she said, "I don't take it unless I have to, and then I spend it first chance I get or I go to the bank and get it changed for new bills. Money like that, you don't know what germs and all it's maybe got on it."

I stuffed the bills into my pocket.

"The last time I had bills like that," I said, "I didn't have to wait till I could spend them or get them changed at the bank. I had them stolen from me almost right away."

Floyd laughed.

"You go waving those around," he said, "they'll get stolen off of you, too."

"I can't understand you people," I said. "You were all too

scared of that poor kid's old man for any of you to open your mouths. Now all of a sudden you're not scared any more."

"The cops have him," Louella said. "There's nothing to be scared of any more. He'll be put away."

"The cops had me and they couldn't make it stick. I had a good lawyer. Suppose it happens the same way with him and he'll be on the loose again."

Louella shrugged and the big man grinned.

"Gus was a dope," he said.

"Because he talked to me? Louella's talking a lot more."

"Not because he talked to you," Parsons explained. "Because he called Hofstetter and told him you knew. He told Hofstetter you made him talk. Anything we're saying to you, it's just between ourselves, between friends. We won't be telling anybody what we talked about and you won't either."

"How do you know he called Hofstetter?" I asked.

"He told us he was going to," Louella said.

"He was afraid you'd tell Hofstetter who talked to you," Parsons added. "He thought he could make Hofstetter understand that he didn't want to tell you anything. You made him."

"And you're sure I won't tell Hofstetter?"

"Once Gus told you, that did it for the crazy loon," Louella said. "Now it doesn't make any difference who talks, not any more, not even to that crazy, it doesn't."

I wasn't believing a word of it and it seemed clear to me that they didn't care whether I believed them or not. There was an obvious pattern to what they were doing. It had begun with Louella feeding me the Hofstetter story, and that had been nothing I had to dig out of her. She had been all too eager to push it at me. It had been something she had to sell.

Then I'd brought out the two tens and that changed everything. It triggered her into yelling for Parsons, and from that moment on the main event had become their effort to keep me where I was, pinned down on that sofa. That they were going on talking Hofstetter was only because they had to talk about something. The main event was their holding me. The question was, Holding me for what?

I moved to test it out. I polished off my drink.

"I should be moving on," I said.

They didn't step away to give me room. Floyd gulped the last of his drink and got rid of his glass. He was freeing both his hands to deal with me. He planted them on my shoulders and rammed me down deeper into the cushions.

"Watch the hands, mister," I said. "I don't like people putting their paws on me."

"You've got to have another drink," Parsons said.

"You can't go walking out of here on one leg," Louella added. "Fix yourself another one."

"Relax, man," Parsons said. "You're among friends."

"She was a kid and she's dead. My friends don't hold still for a thing like that."

"I didn't want to say it," Louella murmured, "but it's your fault she's dead."

"Yeah," Parsons chimed in. "Knowing the way he is, nobody ever messed with her. No guy would come near her until you came along. You're the one who did it."

Louella gave it the generous twist.

"Of course, you didn't know," she said. "Fix yourself another snort."

I poured myself a short one. I was waiting to see how they'd handle it when I finished that one. Louella freshened Floyd's and her own. Outside in the street an auto horn sounded. It was two shorts, a long, and two shorts.

"To friendship," Louella said.

Although she had fixed herself a long drink, she took it down gulp after gulp, chugalugging it until she had the whole thing polished off. Parsons took his down the same way and they both stepped away from me. Suddenly I had moving room. It took only a light shove for me to roll the bar cart out of line.

I tossed my drink off, set my glass on the cart, and pushed it out of the way. They had what they had been holding me for. It was out there in the street, waiting for me. I could guess that Louella had set it up by telephone when she'd had Parsons take over on me so she could go out to get the drinks.

With only the retentive sofa to fight, I made it to my feet.

"Now I must be going," I said. "Thanks for the drinks and thanks for everything."

"Friends?" Parsons said, putting out his hand.

"What else?" I said, as we shook.

"Come again anytime," Louella invited. "Now that we've got to know each other, let's not be strangers."

I put my hand inside my coat and got a good grip on my gun.

"Come out with me and see me to my car," I said.

I fully expected that they would refuse, and I was ready to pull the gun on Parsons and march him out the door in front of me. If I was going to be walking into bullets, he looked like the best shield available.

They didn't refuse.

"Sure thing," Parsons said. "I want a look at those snazzy wheels of yours."

The two of them came along and I didn't have to maneuver anything. They went out the door ahead of me and, walking past the pink mammoth to get to Baby, I had them as a double shield all the way. It gave me a chance to look up and down the street. There was nothing in sight that looked like anything. Of course, there were all kinds of places where a sniper could be holed up in cover and concealment, but they were showing no signs of worry.

I pulled out of the driveway and headed away from the neighborhood. Traffic was heavy. It was the time of day when all over the place parking lots were emptying and workers were driving home. I was sure I had something sitting on my tail but there was no spotting it. There were too many cars. Whenever I hit a traffic light and cars would pull up alongside me, I looked, but everyone I saw looked ordinary and nobody seemed to be taking any particular interest in me. Guys did look at Baby but no more than you could call par for the course.

I made for the turnpike but that was no better. It was all but solid with cars. With Baby's maneuverability I could have done some fancy driving, zipping in and out, switching lanes, but I did none of that. I settled into one lane and I held steady there. I was making myself easy to follow.

I came to the service area that you hit short of the New Brunswick exit and I pulled in there. Baby wasn't low on gas but she did have tank room for a few extra gallons. I had her filled up. When I came back on the road, I saw it. It was an Impala I had noticed in the pack behind me. Now I had a new pack showing in my rearview mirror, but the same Impala was there on my tail.

I left the turnpike by the New Brunswick ramp and the Impala left with me. Since I was driving west into the late-afternoon sun, I could see nothing back there but the glare reflected off the Impala's windshield. I couldn't get a look at the driver. I couldn't even tell if it was one man driving alone or if he was carrying a carload of henchmen. I took Route 1, skirting New Brunswick, and beyond the edges of the town the traffic began to thin out a little. The Impala was still with me, but in the thinner traffic it had dropped back a couple of car lengths.

Just short of the Princeton turnoff I came on the first motel. I passed it by. It was one of the big new ones, and that wasn't what I wanted. I rolled on toward Lawrenceville and I saw what I did want on the wrong side of the road. I had to drive on a quarter of a mile before I could hit a place where I could make the U-turn to come back to it. I made the turn and the Impala came along after me.

Rolling back to the motor court I'd spotted, for the first time I was headed east and I had the setting sun at my back. I was no longer getting glare off the Impala's windshield. I could see the driver. He was alone. At a four-car-length distance I was too far away for catching anything like a small mole on a left cheek, but what I could make out of him could have been a good enough fit for the description I'd had of the man the photographer had found so beautiful.

I pulled in at the motor court and got myself a cabin. It was about what I'd expected. The bed looked lumpy. The air conditioner wheezed. There was a noisy drip from the showerhead and everything reeked of mildew and bug killer. With all of that, however, it was still exactly what I wanted.

It had the isolation needed for a private meeting. If there was to be a meeting, I knew it wouldn't happen unless it could be a private one. When I'd driven in, there hadn't been a car parked by any of the cabins. It was the kind of dump that would never begin to fill up until everything else along the road had the NO VACANCY signs out.

I shut the door but I didn't lock it. Waiting, I stood backed against the wall alongside the door. When the door opened I would be behind it. It wasn't a long wait. The knock came.

"It isn't locked," I said. "Come on in."

There followed several moments of nothing. He was standing out there thinking about it. I waited with gun in hand. Then slowly the doorknob turned. It turned and held and there was another pause. It broke with a bang when he kicked the door open. I caught it and held it ajar waiting for him to come through.

He didn't come. I heard the rattle of gravel outside. I could read that. He'd kicked the door open and jumped back from the doorway, waiting for me to make my move. I didn't. I waited with him. Then he came back into the doorway and I knew he was there. From where I was behind the door I couldn't see him, but I knew from what I could see happening to the light inside the cabin. Sunlight had been flooding in through the open door. When he moved to stand in the doorway, the light inside dimmed. His body was blocking the sunlight.

He came in. I could hear him as he moved around looking for me. There wasn't much looking for him to do. The cabin was small and it had no hiding places. I stowed the gun in the belt of my slacks. Then I shoved the door and it slammed shut. He was across the room, looking for me in the john. Since I'd been moving with the closing door and it wasn't until he'd heard the slam that he whirled about to face me, I was close in on him when he did come around.

He had a gun and he rammed the muzzle into my gut. I'd more than half expected that, but I'd gambled that he wouldn't fire. I had no guarantee that he wouldn't, but I had all the evidence to say it wasn't the way he operated. There was a man in the motor court office who would have seen him come in. The man would hear shots. The man would see him drive away. This was a baby who played it cozier than that.

Counting on the guy's caution, I'd stowed my own gun away. I hadn't wanted to scare him into anything hasty that wouldn't have been part of his plan, and I'd read him right. He didn't squeeze the trigger. He just pushed on the gun, digging the muzzle into me.

"Put your hands on top of your head," he said.

I got them up there. He reached with his free hand and pulled my gun out of my belt. He tossed it onto the bed. Pushing with his gun, he backed me toward the door. I thought we were going riding and I was thinking ahead to when he would be taking on the double job of handling his Impala while he kept me covered.

He wasn't that stupid. He stopped at the door only long enough to lock it and then he backed me away from it, keeping me across the room from the bed where he'd tossed my gun. With his gun still pressed into my gut, he patted me down. He was paying me the compliment of thinking I might be two-gun Erridge.

Satisfied, he backed away from me a step or two, still keeping me covered.

"All right," he said. "Hand them over."

"Hand what over?"

"The two bills."

"You've got them. You swiped them out of my room after you knocked her off."

"Not them, the ones you've got now, the ones you showed Harrison, the ones you showed Louella."

"Those," I said. "Dirty the way they are, there's no telling whose germs they've got on them."

"Don't get smart with me. I want them."

I reached into my pocket and brought out the two tens. He snatched them out of my hand. He tried to keep his gun on me while he examined them, but they needed close scrutiny. He had to take his eyes off me. I kept mine on his gun muzzle. It had to happen and I was waiting for it. Since he wasn't watching it and since he was closely focused on the bills, his gun began wavering, moving just that little bit off aim.

He had me standing backed against what in that cabin passed for a writing desk. There was a tin wastepaper basket standing beside it. I kicked out sideways and hit the basket. It skidded, banging and rattling toward the door. He whirled to bring his gun to bear on the noise. I moved with him, jumping for his gun hand.

I chopped his wrist and the gun dropped. I kicked it away. I was between him and the bed. He lost a moment nursing his wrist. I grabbed my gun up off the bed and leveled it at him.

"Now," I said, "we can talk."

"What do you want?"

"I want in."

He was still holding the tens. He wadded them up and flung them at my face. I reached up with my free hand and fielded them.

"Those aren't anything," he said. "They're just a couple of dirty bills."

"They were good enough to bring you here."

"So what?"

"So I know too much to be left out. I want in."

"You know too much to be left living."

"That's right, but *I'm* holding the gun, and since there's nothing much you can do about it I am going to be left living. I can pick up the phone and call the cops and I can hold you till they come and get you. How much they can do on working up evidence for the job you did last night on the Tavern and on Gus I don't know, but they don't have to get you on two murders. One is enough. The restaurant people out there in Pennsylvania remember you. They'll testify she went out of there with you, and I can clinch the rest of it on what I know and on what Laura told me."

"She didn't know anything."

"She had the two tens."

"She didn't know what they were. She was taking off and she was going only with the bread she could stuff in the pockets of her jeans. She didn't want singles. So she took the tens and left me twenty ones. She never knew what they were."

"But when she knew that you had to get them back, she would begin to know and that was knowing too much for you to let her go on living. You gave her the come-back-baby-I-love-you routine and in the bushes you gave her what she took to be proof of it, and then you killed her before she had time to find out."

"You can't prove any of that."

"The cops can. When they come here and take you in, they'll find the two tens on you and they'll find her fingerprints on them and mine as well. It'll add up for no other way you could have them."

I wasn't at all sure of that. Fingerprints, I understand, are chancy stuff. Not all surfaces take them, and more times than not just in the ordinary course of things they smudge and even rub away, but those bills were old and dirty and gummy and they could have been a great surface for taking and holding prints. He couldn't know whether they were or they weren't. He had to be worried about them.

He was.

"You want in?" he asked.

"What do you think? You've got a good thing going. It's good enough to be worth a couple of killings when that's what it takes to carry it on. I've got you where I want you. I can call the cops and turn you in. If you try anything, I can blow you away. What do you think I'm waiting for?"

"I don't know."

"So I turn you in. What do I get out of it? A good-conduct medal? Your racket gets blown and everybody loses. Deal me in and everybody wins. After all, I figure you owe me. You owe me plenty after the way you've been playing me dirty. So it's up to you. We deal or I call the cops."

"We deal," he said.

I lowered my gun and rammed it back in my belt. I saw his eyes slide toward the corner where I had kicked his gun away. He talked. From time to time I interjected appropriate noises to keep him thinking we were in business and that I was relaxed.

Of course it was gang stuff, and the two tens were like a membership badge. A man who carried them could go anywhere and identify himself to members who'd never even heard of him: They would know some markings that had been put on the bills. In a strange city all he needed to know was which bar to go to. He could just sit there and toy with his money and he'd make contact. The one thing a man could never let himself do was lose them. The gang wouldn't tolerate that.

Salvas hadn't called Hofstetter to tell him I was on my way. He'd called *this* bastard to tell him that I was nosing around and asking about the two tens. What Salvas had told me hadn't mattered, but the fact that he had talked at all did matter. That and the state of terror he'd been in when he reported on me had been taken as sufficient demonstration that he would crack under pressure. He had to be eliminated before he cracked.

Then Chief Harrison had reported that I was flourishing the two tens. Yes, he was in it, too, and from that time on it had only been a question of when they could get to me safely. Louella's call set it up for him. She told him they had me and would hold me for him.

He didn't say it, but it was obvious that he'd made a mistake in letting me lead him out of the area where Chief Harrison had jurisdiction. Where we were in Mercer County, there would be no police connection that would do anything for him.

As he talked, he started moving around, taking a few steps toward his gun and then turning around and coming back. He was working at making it look as though he was just pacing the floor, but his eyes kept sliding toward the corner where his gun lay on the floor. I was working along with him, sprawling on the hard lumps of the bed, making myself look more and more relaxed.

He started on Laura and most of that was sex talk, and all the time he was watching to see what it was doing to me. I faked it and gave him what he wanted, all the evidence of prurient fascination. Maybe I even drooled a bit.

He went on and on about how she had been a virgin and a man didn't get much of that these days. He had married her and nobody had known about it but the two of them and some justice of the peace and a couple of professional witnesses in one of those quickie villages down in Maryland.

"The way her old man raised her crazy, she wouldn't unless we were married."

He'd gone through with it but it hadn't meant anything to him. He wasn't the marrying kind. He'd gone on playing the field and Laura had taken it hard.

"She had the crazy idea a guy could only want one. So I was with somebody else a night, she figured it had to be I didn't want her. She took off."

And that was all right with him. He'd never wanted for women and he never would, but she'd taken the two tens.

"Maybe she took them like she said," he told me. "Just so she'd have a smaller roll to carry, but maybe she knew something and she took them to hold them over me. I couldn't take any chance on it and I couldn't leave them floating around."

"Of course you couldn't," I said.

I worked at relaxing some more.

All the time he'd been stepping up the radius of his pacing. He stretched it to the corner, did a quick squat and came up with the gun. He whirled and fired at where I'd been sprawled, but while he was grabbing his gun I'd been rolling across the bed. He moved to take new aim but I was a moving target and, before he could get his gun on me, I squeezed my shot off.

I didn't try for anything fancy like shooting the gun out of his hand. Don't let anyone tell you handguns can be that accurate. I aimed for his body and that did it. A slug fired at close range can hit a man anywhere and it'll knock him off his feet. I got him in the shoulder and, since he'd been firing from his crouch, it caught him when he had minimum stability. The slug knocked him flat and the gun went flying out of his hand.

I picked it up and went to the phone.

I didn't have to make the call. The shots brought the man out of the motor court office. He came on the run. He got through to the police for me. I know they moved right along and added Chief Harrison and Louella and Floyd to the bag. I believe they also got some others in the gang. They say they busted up the whole organization, which may or may not be true. Anyhow, that's their department. Mine covered the murder of Lolita-Laura, nothing more.